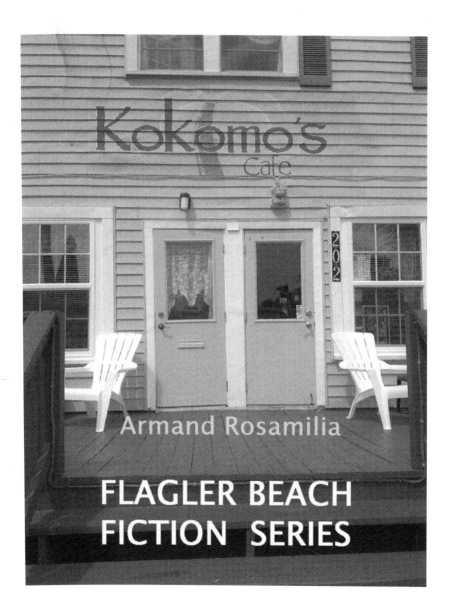

Armand Rosamilia

FLAGLER BEACH
FICTION SERIES

KOKOMO'S CAFÉ

Flagler Beach Fiction Series

Armand Rosamilia

Edited by Jenny Adams

Cover and Interior Photos by David Royall

Rymfire Books

http://armandrosamilia.com

Print Edition July 2013

Special Thanks to Mark and Tina Hutsell for the generous help and the great coffee and food from Kokomo's Café

David Royall for the great pictures of Kokomo's Café and Jenny Adams for the great editing job... I owe both of you (as usual)

And the many varied characters that make up the unique sunny paradise that is Flagler Beach

Flagler Beach Fiction Series

Kokomo's Café

Golden Lion Cafe

J And J Fitness

Flagler Fish Company

Nerdz Comics And More

Sully's Surf Shop

Bahama Mama's

Kokomo's Café

Flagler Fiction Series

Be Here In The Mornin'

Three people, with tired eyes and dry mouths, were standing on the front deck, waiting for Mac to open. The same three he saw each and every weekday. It was the start of another Kokomo's Café morning.

"Good morning, Dean." Mac smiled at the older man, his wisps of gray hair flapping in the gentle breeze. Dean owned one of the knickknack stores dotting A1A, selling anything he could squeeze FLAGLER BEACH onto: shot glasses, shirts, flip flops, banners, and beach towels. He even had it stamped onto the ice cream in the cooler. "The usual?"

Dean grunted.

Not a morning person, Mac thought. No matter. He'd take his spot at the big window across from the counter and finger through the newspaper while the coffee was brewing.

The woman was named Beverly. She was a prominent local realtor, coming in for her morning double shot of espresso and a blueberry muffin. She'd ask Mac if he was ever going to sell his house in Palm Coast so she could get him a deal and he'd laugh it off. Of course, if his wife Ginny was opening with him, she'd be all ears. Her dream was to sell the big house and move to Flagler Beach so they could be near the café and the beach.

Mac started up the coffee, hitting the lights in the kitchen and preparing whatever he needed for the opening. Ginny would be here by nine with ice and more coffee, which they'd need for the busy weekend ahead, especially with the farmer's market going on across the street in Veteran's Park.

The third member of the morning visitors (Mac liked to refer to them as the Breakfast Club) was the large guy who sat at the corner table, head down, staring intently at his laptop. He wore black t-shirts with humorous/almost-offensive slogans and only took breaks for phone calls, a refill of his coffee and to order lunch. He stayed through the morning and left around two. Mac didn't know who he was but he was someone, because people came in to talk with him and sometimes met him for lunch.

Mac went to work on Beverly's wake-me-up as the fresh coffee brewed. He had a system and it was running like clockwork right now.

Then the front door opened at the same time the back door did.

It's going to be a busy morning, he thought. "Good morning, how's it going?"

A young couple, in swimwear under long white shirts, came in from the front. They were smiling and couldn't keep their hands off each other. They ordered cappuccino and egg and cheese sandwiches. The older woman, coming in from the back steps, was still going through the menu, even though it was a simple folded sheet with a handful of items.

When Mac saw the couple looking around as they stood and waited for their food, he pointed at the nearest table. "You guys can sit anywhere you like, in here or in the side room, or outside. I'll be happy to bring your sandwiches out to you."

She smiled. "Let's sit outside at a picnic table. It's so nice today."

Mac went to the kitchen and started getting orders together, trying to stay ahead until Ginny got into work. They'd been open for business since October, and the customer base had grown considerably in the last eight or nine months. The couple had been lucky so far, and Mac knew the café had a great vibe to it and great food, which had the locals coming back for more. Now that summer was here, the tourists were trickling in. Some of the snow birds decided to stick around town longer than usual, and Fourth of July would be a huge event in Flagler Beach, with fireworks just off the pier and the town jammed with families.

Mac and Ginny had run 100-seat restaurants in the past, but he'd sworn never again. He loved the one on one Kokomo's Café afforded him. He liked serving one person at a time, being able to take a break during slow periods and sitting out in the dining area and shooting the shit with the locals. The view from the big window was wonderful: today and tomorrow he would have a good view of the farmer's market, with people coming and going and, occasionally, stopping in to get coffee or a muffin. This was small town at its core, and he loved being situated so close to it and being a part of it.

He was only a block from the Atlantic Ocean, and the view past Veterans Park, the palm trees and parked cars was of clear blue skies dipping into a gorgeous body of water, pure and sparkling in the morning sunlight.

The back door opened and Mac popped his head out, saying hello to two men who came in. *Yep, busy busy day, so far.* Mac started moving at double speed to keep up, and he loved the challenge.

"Hello, how are you?" Mac heard Ginny as she came through the front door, greeting everyone as she came into the kitchen. She was good with names, and often reminded her husband who was who. Without her, everyone would be Ma'am and Buddy.

She came around the counter and took the order of the two men, slapping the slip down next to Mac. "I guess you've been busy."

"So far, I can't complain. I'm just glad you're in and here early. If they kept wandering in, it might've gotten a little hairy." Mac snuck a quick kiss to his wife's cheek and returned her smile.

Ginny went back out to the front and Mac heard her greet Beverly, by name, which meant, during a lull, the two would be talking about the best way to sell their house, the money they could expect, and how to get Mac to agree to it. They both knew he wasn't going to sell the house, but it was part of the game they played.

Mac wondered what they'd say if he told them he'd thought about it, and they should sell the house and move back to California, selling Kokomo's and pulling up all ties to this area. Ginny would have a cow.

He was still chuckling to himself when he ran out the first sandwiches to customers. Ginny was filling coffee cups and chatting with everyone.

The young couple outside was too busy staring into each other's eyes to give him more attention than a brief thank you. *Ah, to be that young and in love*, he mused. Mac went back inside and Ginny winked at him.

"Maybe being old and in love isn't so bad," he mumbled.

"Did you say something?"

Mac stopped and returned the wink. After more than twenty-five years of marriage, they still had the spark. She was still his soul-mate and the love of his life. Things were good. But, right now, they were busy.

"Just keep the orders piling up and I'll get back into the kitchen," he said. He loved it when they were busy, not only for the obvious reason, they were making money, but because he could get on a roll and enjoy the creation of a good sandwich.

Mac finished the orders, floated food baskets to tables, handed out bags of Lay's original or barbeque chips, and refilled two coffee cups. And he did it all with a grin and a chuckle, because he was having a good time.

He walked outside to the back porch, cradling a cigarette in his hand. It was time for a quick drag before they got busy again. He stood and admired the perfect weather of Flagler Beach, and the small town feel of the place. Like no other. Mac lit his cigarette and leaned against the rail, watching the people coming and going at the farmer's market. He'd need to run over, at some point this morning, and get red onions, field greens and fresh tomatoes.

The owner of the Salty Dog stepped out from his tiny restaurant and gave a quick wave before resetting his outside tables and chairs, expecting a late morning crowd, hungry for his daily specials after shopping at the farmer's market. Mac liked the guy (he might be named Billy, but Mac was horrible with names) and watched him as he worked. Just like Mac and Ginny, Billy and his wife owned the Salty Dog and did all the cooking, serving and smiling, themselves.

"This is the life, right?" Andrew 'Woody' Woodson said, as if reading Mac's mind, coming up the steps to the back deck. He smiled, his thick black glasses bouncing as he laughed. "Gotta love this weather." He peeked around Mac through the open door. "You got busy early today. Sweet."

"Yeah, I can't complain." Mac took a long last drag on his cigarette. "You hungry?'

"You buying?"

"Nope."

Woody laughed. "I'll have a fried egg on a roll and some of your strongest and cheapest coffee. I need to wake up, big night tonight."

Mac nodded and motioned for Woody to go inside. "First Friday events are always fun and we have great weather for it. We'll stay open late and stay busy."

Woody seemed to know everyone in Kokomo's Café, nodding and acknowledging everyone by name. He was the main bartender at the Golden Lion, having run the tiki bar for the past six years. Woody knew everyone in town, and everyone knew him. He was the local celebrity, with his quick smile and flirty attitude toward anything female. Woody played the part and he played it well. Mac thought it must be exhausting to have to play the part twenty-four-seven. You couldn't step outside your front door without having to play a character, a bigger than life version of who you really were.

Back in the kitchen, Mac stretched before taking over for Ginny. While she had no problem fixing orders, he loved her upfront, dealing with customers, while he ruled the kitchen. He liked to create, and loved the challenge of coming up with a new item for the special's board.

When he took the new order out and put it down on a table, he heard Beverly and Ginny talking about their house and what they could get for it.

"I'm telling you, I have a buyer who would scoop up your house for two-fifty five. Easy. It's in a great neighborhood and right on the corner and I know Mac has everything in top working condition and it's an inspector's dream."

Mac put his head down and went back to the kitchen to await his next sandwich, feeling hungry himself. It was about time to make breakfast. "Honey, you want a fried egg and bacon sandwich while I'm making one?"

"Sounds good." Ginny stepped into the doorway. "While we have a break, why don't you come out and talk to Beverly and me?"

Mac frowned. He was still rolling around the dollar amount Beverly had casually kicked out there, and knew she'd said it so he could hear the price. It was impressive; he had to admit. He'd paid one hundred sixty five years ago, with most of it down in cash. He didn't owe much more. But his argument was always simple: why not pay off the house and then own it and not worry? How many people ever get to the point where they pay off a mortgage, and within half the time or less?

But he didn't want to sell the house. He liked it, which was the reason he bought it in the first place. His entire adult life had been about saving money, doing the right thing, and running his own business and building his nest egg and savings account so his two kids could go to college and he and Ginny would be set when they got older.

"I'm busy," Mac finally said, and went back to his work, cutting tomatoes that didn't need to be touched right now.

"Suit yourself," Ginny said. "When you're done doing your busy work so you don't have to talk to me, can I get that sandwich?"

Mac grinned but turned away from her. Damn, the woman knew him too well. "Of course, honey."

*　*　*　*　*

"I'm dead serious," Beverly said and put on her best realtor smile.

Mac knew exactly what she was doing. He didn't like being seen, by her, as dollar signs and another potential sale but knew she was doing her job. Mac pushed away from the table and Ginny reached over and put her hand softly on his.

The place was quiet, with everyone sitting and eating and no one needing a refill on coffee or another order at the moment. Mac liked these breaks, because then he could steal a glance at the weather on the television and get a cup of water or coffee for himself. Sitting here, listening to Beverly trying to buy his house and put them into one right on the beach, and pocketing about twenty grand to boot, wasn't what he'd signed up for when he crawled out of bed this morning.

Mac looked at Ginny, who was smiling. He shrugged his shoulders. "What do you want me to do?"

"I just want you to listen to what she's saying."

Mac looked at Beverly. "This all sounds really wonderful and fun, but can you back it up? Put your money where your mouth is?"

"If you are serious. I have the perfect place for you to look at, six blocks from here. Two stories, great view of the ocean from the balcony."

"I already have a great view of the ocean." Mac looked out the big window at the Atlantic, only two blocks away, past the farmer's market and the park. He had come to love Flagler Beach since moving here, and Kokomo's Café was a dream come true. The locals embraced them as family, and he'd met so many friends since opening a few short months ago. The drive, while only taking twenty minutes, was sometimes a pain to him. Twenty more minutes of sleep? Mac didn't hate the idea.

"We could walk to work," Ginny said.

Mac tapped on his growing gut and sighed. "Now you're calling me fat."

"I always call you fat. I like your old man belly you're getting, like my own little pot-bellied pig."

Beverly covered her mouth and snorted.

"Perfect. I'm fat and a pig now."

Ginny rubbed her husband's shoulder. "I say it all with love in my heart and humor in my words."

"But more humor."

"Of course." Ginny hugged him.

"What does the house even look like?" Mac turned to Ginny. "Did you see it already? Without me?"

"No, I swear. I'm waiting for you and I to go see it… tonight, after we close."

"Wow. You two are good." Mac stood when the front door opened and a young woman with her two children came in. He greeted them and tried to slip around to the back of the café before Ginny said another word.

"Is that a yes?" she called out.

Mac went to the counter and greeted the woman and her children, took their order and told them to have a seat inside or out, and he'd bring the food to them. He pointedly ignored his wife and the realtor, going out of his way to start the order in the kitchen.

Beverly rose from her chair and leaned over the counter. "Thanks for the breakfast, Mac. I'll see you tonight, or I'll see you in the morning. Either way, it was fun, as usual."

"You have a great day. I'll see you soon," Mac yelled, hoping it was cryptic enough and would drive Ginny crazy.

It worked. She was next to him, in the kitchen, before he had time to pull the bread out. He was fighting the laugh in his throat.

"No fair and you know it. I have no patience. Why are you doing this? I think it's a great chance for us, and the kids will be gone to college and their own lives soon, and we need to start thinking about our future together. Just the two of us." Ginny hugged Mac from behind and put her chin near his ear. "Imagine waking up in the morning."

"That would be nice. Waking up is always a bonus."

Ginny squeezed him. "Shush and let me wow you with my feminine charms."

"Heck, you might as well just paw at my manhood and be done with it, then. You know how easy I am."

"I'd rather get you excited about the house and not just excited."

"Both would be nice, you know. We could sneak into the walk-in freezer and go at it like teenagers."

Ginny laughed in his ear. "We don't have a walk-in."

"Note to self: buy a walk-in freezer."

"You're so silly." Ginny released and turned her husband around. "Can we at least look at the house on the beach?"

The bell over the back door rang.

Mac smiled. "Of course. Right after work. Just let Beverly know."

Ginny kissed him on the cheek. "She already does, silly."

Girls On The Beach

"I'll give you fifty bucks if you take your shirt off."

"Not a chance," Michael Zaun said to his lovable but annoying buddy, Larry, as they stepped inside Kokomo's Café. Larry was always trying to get him to do stupid things or dares he knew Michael wouldn't accept. Taking off his shirt at the beach? It wasn't going to happen and it didn't matter what the offer was.

"One hundred dollars. Final offer."

"Shut up." Michael stepped to the counter and looked at the special's board. "I'll take a coffee."

Ginny smiled at the two men. "Leave room for cream and sugar?"

"Yes, ma'am."

"I'll have the same," Larry said. He turned to Michael. "But I'm not going to *ma'am* her. That's just rude."

"No, it's not. It's a sign of respect."

"She's not that much older than you."

"Age has nothing to do with respect. If the person is friendly, I will be respectful. It has nothing to do with anything else," Michael said.

Ginny leaned across the counter and handed them two coffee cups. "There you go, *sir*." Ginny smiled and winked at Michael. "And I might be old enough to be your mom."

"Doubt it," Larry said and flashed a grin. "You don't look that old."

Michael elbowed his friend. "Don't hit on her. You're so embarrassing."

"She's cute. You know I love older women."

The pair added cream and sugar to their coffees; Larry with a smile and Michael with a frown.

They went outside and sat on one of the light blue picnic benches.

"It is gorgeous out here," Larry said. "Too bad your grandfather's farm isn't closer."

"It's not that far," Michael said defensively. "Less than a two hour drive."

"Still too far. But I like this better than the beach we went to last week, even though it was a drive across Jacksonville." Larry sighed. "Maybe someday I'll buy a place out here and settle down, have a few kids, get me an older wife who cooks and cleans, and retire."

"You work so hard now," Michael said.

Larry had gotten lucky during the internet boom of the late 1990's, creating a torrent site to cull pornography into one easy-to-use interface. Then, at its peak, Larry sold it and turned the money into stocks and other investments. He was in his late twenties and would never have to work a day in his life. Now, he drifted through life and rented nice houses in New York and New Jersey, where they'd grown up together, but never for more than a year at a time because he got bored.

"How long are you planning on staying?" Michael asked him.

Larry looked up and down South Central Street and shrugged. "As long as I want, I guess. You're sick of me here already?"

"I'm always sick of you."

"I was thinking of heading to Miami or Key West soon. We should go, maybe bring Susan and Becky with us."

Susan was their friend, four years younger than Michael. He'd had a weird relationship with her so far, not knowing if she just wanted to be friends or more than that. He sure as heck wasn't going to push it and do the wrong thing. Becky was Susan's mom, in her forties, and Larry was quite smitten with her. She was funny and beautiful, and loved the attention Larry gave her.

Larry, who Michael called the Porn King because of the website... his best friend, was also a virgin. Just like Michael. At least Larry had something going for him, with all his money and a tall, thin body. Michael was a big guy.

I'm actually obese, he thought. Sitting out in the sun, even under the umbrella over the table, was killing him. But he refused to take off his shirt or wear shorts because of his size. He'd lost a few pounds recently, and tried to get up early each morning and walk the Zaun Farm, but he never went far before getting tired.

Knowing he was going to depress himself if he kept thinking about shit like this, he sipped his coffee and followed Larry's gaze. "What about here?"

"What about it?"

"This would be a sweet town to settle down in for a year."

"You are trying to get rid of me," Larry said.

"I never said I wasn't. You've been mooching off of me for weeks. I'm just wondering when you're going to split." In truth, Michael was glad his friend had stayed so long. He helped fix up the farm, and was a constant companion. The locals out in rural Jacksonville hadn't been overly friendly to Michael, especially when they found out he was living at Zaun Farm, the sight of the Tool Shed Murders, committed by Michaels' grandfather. "By this time, you get antsy and take off."

"I'm going to. I just said I'll be heading south. I want you to come with me."

"I need to find a job."

"No, you don't. You collect rent from the properties on your land, and you know damn well you've been sinking money into the farm because you're bored. You could easily live off the money coming in, and selling off another ten acres will net you some big bucks. You might not have money like me, but you're doing well. I'll help you invest a couple of bucks and you won't have to work again. Then we can travel."

"You do know I like women, right? And you're too skinny."

"I'm not quite sure what you really like, dude. If I were you, I'd be nailing Susan like a real man."

"You mean like you're banging away at her mom?"

Larry chuckled. "I'm taking my sweet time with her. I'm a gypsy, a nomad. I don't want her falling in love with me and then having to crush her spirit. I've done it too many times to mention."

"I don't remember that ever happening. In fact, if I remember correctly, the closest you've ever gotten besides all the porn…"

Larry put his hands up. "Enough. It doesn't matter. I'm thinking I'll be heading somewhere soon. Really soon, I think."

"Miami or the Keys?"

"Maybe Tampa. Have you ever been to Tampa?"

"I haven't been anywhere in Florida, except with you."

"I thought you came to Florida, as a kid, to your grandfather's farm?"

"Yes, and we stayed around town and the farm."

"Then we need to go to Tampa."

"What's in Tampa?"

Larry shrugged. "Shit we haven't seen yet. We can head south from there and visit Sarasota and Fort Myers. Wherever else is interesting. Stay in hotels or rent a camper, do some traveling before I leave."

"Why would you leave? Look around. This place is awesome. I'll never go back north and shovel another snowflake. I came down on a whim but now I know it's the best thing I've ever done in my life. You should think about staying."

"I can't. You know me. I get bored too easily. I like Florida; I might hang around for a bit and see everything there is to see, but I won't be here for more than a year."

A huge biker dude and a young girl, probably his daughter, walked up and went up the stairs and inside Kokomo's Café.

"Shut up," Michael said.

"What?"

"I'm sure you're going to say something stupid, or offer me money to do something dumb."

"It's not dumb unless you don't do it."

"I'm not going to do anything to that guy, so forget it."

"Not even for a hundred dollars?"

"Not even for a thousand."

Larry rubbed the stubble on his cheek. "What if I offered you ten grand?"

"First, you don't have ten grand in cash on you, and I would never take a check. Second... no."

"Go inside and tell him you think all bikers are stupid."

"For ten grand?"

"And then slap him in the face."

"And then get killed. No thanks."

"You were thinking about it."

"No, I wasn't. Not for a second." Michael would have actually thought about it if it was only to say something idiotic to the guy, since he could then tell him it was a joke and it was for money and he'd pray for the biker not to kill him. Regardless, Larry would laugh his ass off and it would be worth the money to have another damn story to tell.

"I'd love to go to New Orleans someday," Michael said, to change the subject.

"Wow, what a coincidence: Susan was talking about it the other night. With you. I wonder if she has anything to do with it? You probably didn't even know about NOLA before she said it."

"NOLA?"

"That's what the cool people call New Orleans."

"Then why are you?"

Larry shrugged. "I'm not really sure."

* * * * *

"Man, this is a divine sign, and you know it."

"Leave me alone and let me play in the water," Michael said to Larry. They were standing under the Flagler Pier, out of the sun, and Michael was taking baby steps into the surf. He wanted to get his feet wet but there was no way he was going in deeper than his ankles. His jeans were pulled up but the cuffs were wet already.

Larry, in shorts, spinning his shirt in his hand and showing off his pasty-white torso, was running through the waves like a little kid. "I'm telling you, I will give you fifty bucks if you run over there and knock him down. Better yet, kick sand in his face."

"He's standing up, and he's, like, two feet taller than me. That makes no sense."

It was the biker and his daughter (at least, Michael hoped it was his daughter, since she was likely less than half his age), and while she played in the ocean like Larry, the biker was standing on the beach in his jeans and biker boots, sunglasses down, and talking on a cell phone.

"Alright, how about a hundred bucks to knock him down and another hundred to kick sand in his beard?"

"You offered me ten thousand to smack him not even an hour ago."

"And you didn't do it, so we start over again."

"I'll do it for twenty grand," Michael said.

Larry stopped jumping around. "Seriously?"

Michael had to really think about it. He'd thrown out the huge number in jest, but now Larry was taking the bait. Shit. He looked at the biker, who was a monster. He was like an extra from *Sons of Anarchy*, a scary mountain of a man. The lyrics to the New Jersey band Fountains Of Wayne song "Leave the Biker" came to his mind, and he knew he'd be stuck with it for the rest of the weekend. Only, in his reality, this dude would squash him like a grape.

Larry walked over and put his arm around Michael. The two stared at the man as he talked on the phone, which could barely be seen in his overlarge hand.

"This guy could give Andre the Giant a run for his money."

"Andre is dead."

"Not the point. This man would give Thunderlips a run for his money."

"Thunderlips?"

Larry nodded sagely. "Hulk Hogan in the *Rocky* movie, remember?"

"Only you would know something as stupid as that."

They stopped talking as the girl ran out of the surf and joined the biker before heading back toward the steps and the pier.

"She's kinda cute," Larry said. "But way too young for me."

"Bea Arthur is too young for you," Michael said.

"There is a line, and she might be just over it. I can't help it if I like MILFs."

"You like GMILFs. That's the problem. It's creepy."

"Hey, if a fifty year old mama happens to have grandkids, it's not my problem. Those kids aren't going to ever call me Grandpa Larry."

"I really hope so."

"He's getting away. Last chance to earn fifty bucks."

"Twenty grand was my asking price," Michael said.

"A hundred bucks to go grab her ass."

"Then he'll really kill me. I'd rather trip him for twenty large."

"You sound like such a thug when you talk like that. You've been listening to N.W.A. again?"

"Yeah, found a torrent with every song any member of N.W.A. has ever released. Pretty cool."

"Especially for a white guy who won't even take off his shirt on the beach."

"I'm not going to do it."

The friends watched the biker and the girl disappear onto the boardwalk above them.

"Twenty bucks to take your shirt off."

"Why do you want to see my man-boobs so bad?"

Larry shrugged. "I just want to see if you'll do it. Wander up and down the beach without a shirt on."

"You offered me fifty before."

"No, I didn't. Will you do it for fifty?"

Maybe I Don't Know

Charlie Newman ordered two hot teas.

"Leave room for cream and sugar?" Mac asked with a smile.

"Has anyone ever told you that you look like Billy Joel?"

Mac laughed. "I get it at least once a day. I wish I had his money."

Charlie turned and looked at Edith, who was sitting at the table near the front window. "You need room for cream and sugar?"

Edith turned and faced him with a sour look on her face. "What do you think?"

Charlie had no idea, because he didn't really pay attention to stupid things like what she put in her tea. They'd been dating for a little over two years but he didn't make a mental inventory of every food she liked or hated, or what she put in her coffee or tea. He didn't remember if she even liked coffee.

He was too old for shit like this. Last weekend was his fifty-third birthday. Not that Edith had done anything special for him. She was actually mad his kids had taken him to Alfie's in Ormond Beach for his special day. Edith and Charlie went to the Golden Lion for dinner and drinks on Saturdays. He'd thrown off their routine by celebrating a birthday.

Charlie shrugged at Mac. "Leave room in both, I guess." He knew he wanted cream and sugar. He looked at Edith again, who was back to staring straight ahead and frowning at the paintings on the wall.

Mac leaned over the counter. "She likes a little cream and a lot of sugar."

"Thanks. One day I'll remember." *And one day maybe I'll even care*, Charlie thought. He took his time, putting cream and sugar in both cups and securing the lids. Every Friday he came to Kokomo's Café with her, getting two teas and sitting in the same seats and watching people come and go in silence, until it was time for her to leave. He didn't understand the point of these Friday late morning dates, but Edith insisted. Charlie could count on one hand how many words they'd spoken since they started coming here, in the last six months or so.

He held both cups over the table between them, looking around for the daily newspaper. He wouldn't actually be able to read it until she left, but he wanted to get an idea where it was, currently, and who was reading it. Once Edith ran off, he could order a slice of cake (she watched everything he ate, like a hawk, and was quick to comment how fattening things were, even though she could stand to lose more than a few pounds).

"We need to talk," she said, in almost a whisper, startling him, as he put down the cups of tea. He looked around, expecting another person to be near them. Surely, it wasn't him she needed to talk to. He sat down.

Charlie took a sip of his tea and stared out the window at the young couple sitting outside, at a table under an umbrella, enjoying the breeze off the Atlantic Ocean. He preferred coffee, and never drank tea except on Fridays. It was easier ordering two teas and getting through it than dealing with Edith.

He wondered if they were newlyweds, flying down from some far-off place in the Midwest but unable to afford Hawaii or Key West. Just a couple of young kids with a full life ahead, thinking they'd met their dream companion, and they'd spend the next fifty years in wedded bliss. Charlie wanted to go out there and punch them both in the face. Knock some sense into them.

"Are you listening to me?"

"Of course," Charlie said and plastered a smile on his face. "I'm always listening."

"You're always antsy, fidgeting around and staring into space. I don't think you hear a word I say."

"Of course I do." *I hear them in my sleep... in my nightmares.* He asked himself, for the twentieth time today alone, why he was with her. Why did he take this crap? Why did he even care to waste his life in this endless routine of being bullied and put down by this heartless woman?

"Then what did I say?"

He'd already forgotten, lost in his thoughts about her never shutting up and always nagging. "We always play this game. Can't we move the conversation along?"

She looked like he'd smacked her across her makeup-caked face. "Excuse me?"

Charlie put his head down, gripping his cup. "Is your tea good?"

Edith put both hands on the table, and he stared at her thin, vein-riddled fingers, so pale they were nearly translucent. She was like a ghost, flittering around, haunting him. *Maybe she is dead, and this is my hell*, Charlie thought. *It would be heaven if I had something to do with her death, though.*

"Well?" Edith asked.

"Well, what?"

She threw her hands up in obvious frustration, her palms slapping the table and putting the room into temporary silence. "I asked you a direct question."

"Direct it at me again, please." He was feeling feisty today, and wasn't in the mood for this. Charlie decided another silent day would have been better. Then she would have left and he could have gotten some food and coffee.

"I don't chew my cabbage twice," she said and sighed.

Charlie remembered she'd said that a few times over the last couple of years, and he thought it meant she didn't repeat herself, but he couldn't be sure. It was a stupid way of saying *I won't say it again.*

"I don't like cabbage, but bread and fry some zucchini and I'm happy. When was the last time you cooked?"

Edith's frown was even more prominent now. Charlie tried to picture her smiling and failed. When was the last time she'd been happy? Laughed? Gotten laid? It sure wasn't with him.

Charlie couldn't remember if Edith had ever cooked for him. Their relationship consisted of eating out and a steady, boring routine.

"I am talking about us. Where this relationship is headed, and why your kids are animals."

Charlie sipped his tea and sighed. "Did you ever think, when you were in your teens or even your twenties, at your age, you'd still be trying to figure out love and relationships and sex and just being nice to another person?"

Edith slid her chair back and Charlie thought she was going to get up and leave, but instead she'd done it for the drama. She was good at it. "What are you trying to say? Don't even think of turning this around. Your children were at my house the last time and now one of my glasses are missing."

"You have plastic cups."

Edith looked enraged. "The actual price of the cup isn't the point."

"Fifteen cents, at the Dollar General, right now."

"What?"

He'd confused her and Charlie smiled to himself. He loved throwing her off-guard. *Small victories and all that*, he thought. He wondered why she even bothered talking to him, because he would usually shut her up with one of his unfiltered comments. Nothing ever rude, but he liked to think he kept her guessing and kept her quiet.

"Plastic cups are on sale. When you leave here, head over. I'll give you two bucks. You can buy a dozen of them." Charlie couldn't help it; he actually smiled.

Edith gripped her coffee cup. The look in her eyes made him put his hand up, waiting for her to douse him with hot tea and cause a scene. Instead, Edith seemed to compose herself and put her hands in her lap. "The price of the cups isn't the point. The fact one of your animal kids or their animal children came into my home and stole from me is the point. And it was my favorite green and yellow one, too. Buying new cups isn't going to solve the real problem. "

"I'm not sure what the real problem is, besides a missing green and yellow plastic cup."

"The point. I don't want anyone from your family in my house."

"I don't think it will even be an issue." Charlie's daughter had complained the last time they were there how rude Edith was to her two kids, and how Edith spent the day yelling at them to stop touching her stuff and to sit still. Edith didn't own a television, despite living in a million dollar home in Hammock Beach and being filthy rich. She cut coupons from the paper and wouldn't buy name brands or leave anything bigger than a twenty percent tip.

"It's not that I hate them… not all of them… but I can't have the integrity of my safety breached."

Charlie had no idea what that even meant, but nodded. Sometimes Edith showed off her big vocabulary. She was a teacher or principal or professor before she retired. He didn't quite remember. In any event, she was smart and looked down on his upbringing and his years in the construction business. Charlie worked with his hands his entire life, and, even at his age, he looked healthy and in shape. Not soft and sluggish like Edith. He was sure her husband had been some rich guy and never worked an honest day in his life, and then died early from too many rich foods and sitting around, counting his piles of money. Now this bitch was reaping the rewards. And she wasn't going to part with it anytime soon, either.

Not that he was interested in it. He had his own money, and prided himself on working for a living and earning every red cent he had. Nothing was free, and he'd instilled this in his own kids. They never asked for money because they knew the answer would be no. Work and manage your own shit, and get through life on your own. Never put your hand out, unless it was to take a job or a paycheck you busted your ass earning.

"They are all guilty by association. Until the culprit comes forward and admits they stole from me, and then is subsequently banned from my property, they will all be unwelcome in my home. Is this understood?"

"Sure, sure, whatever." Charlie's tea was getting cold. He didn't like tea to begin with, but cold it was gross. He sucked it down in two gulps. He didn't think there was a holiday coming up this summer he'd need to gather everyone for, anyway. By the fall, this stupidity will have been forgotten. He didn't know who stole the plastic cup and he really didn't care. Why was she dwelling on it? Maybe one of the little ones had juice in it. Maybe she misplaced it, or one of her annoying dogs chewed it up. There could be a million reasons, but she was honing in on his kids and grandkids being in her house. "I'll give you the two bucks."

"You never listen to me. I already said it wasn't about the price of the cup or replacing it. I have more money than you'll ever see in a lifetime. You never listen."

"I am listening." Charlie wanted to bolt from his seat. How much more of this interrogation would he be forced to take? "All I do is listen to you. I listen to you moan. I listen to you complain. I listen to you bitch."

"Did you just call me a bitch?"

Charlie sighed. "No, I said you bitched. There's a difference." But he did think she was a major bitch.

"I don't see the difference. This is getting ridiculous." Edith pointed a finger at his face. "You need to get your crap together, do you understand? I'm not going to do this for the rest of my life. It's not worth it. What's in this for me? Where is the big payoff on my end? You're the one reaping all the rewards. I get nothing but attitude, indifference and ignorance."

"Maybe we should break up," Charlie muttered.

"What did you say?"

He thought about it. He'd spit it out automatically, but it did make sense to him. A lot of sense. What was in this for Charlie? She had all this money but he was the one paying for tea and dinner every time they went out. He tried to remember the last time she paid for anything and he couldn't. He was the money-pit in the relationship, but she was going to complain?

"I guess you got what you wanted from me. I gave you the money to fix your van, and now you don't need me anymore. Is that it?"

Oh, yeah, she did pay to get the van fixed, but only because my unemployment deposit was late with the holiday, Charlie thought. He'd need to pay her back soon to shut her up. "I'm starting to really dislike the person you've become," he finally said when she wouldn't stop staring at him. It was the line his third ex-wife had used on him before she kicked him out.

"I haven't changed," Edith said and then her lips curled on one side. "But neither have you, and that's the problem. I thought I'd be able to whip you into shape. So far, you're like a lump of clay drying up, flaking off, and falling apart. I think I just need to dig my fingers in deeper and find the soft spots to get you into the proper form."

Charlie started to stand. "I'm going to get coffee."

"Sit down. You drink tea when you're with me."

Charlie sat.

"Are we clear about your animal family?"

"I wish you'd stop calling them that."

"What would you call them?"

Charlie shrugged. "My family would suffice, no?"

"Not in this case." Edith closed her eyes and sighed. When she opened them, she fixed Charlie with such an intense stare he tried to look away, but she had him locked. "I need you to talk less and listen more. Can you do that?"

"Sure, why not?" Charlie just wanted to get away but he was unable to move. He suddenly felt like he was stuck in a web, and the spider was sipping tea across the table from him. His mind screamed at his legs to step away and start running for the exit like he was on fire, but they wouldn't obey. He stared blankly at Edith, awaiting the next words from her mouth. A mouth like a tarantula.

"Today, I'm not going to leave first. I usually have to go down to Java Joint and get a cup of coffee and something to eat, but I feel like trying one of the sandwiches here. They smell and look good. It's going to be your turn to leave and find somewhere else to eat. I suggest Java Joint, or The Beach House Beanery. But no cake. Eat healthy for a change. You just aren't going to stay here. I think it would be fair, every other time we meet at Kokomo's, you can stay and I will go."

Charlie finished his tea, which was now cold. He was tired. Maybe he'd skip eating today and just go back to his daughter's rental (he slept on her couch) and take a nap before her animal kids got home from school. "Is our date done?"

Edith glanced at her watch. "Yes. I will see you tomorrow night at Golden Lion. Don't be late. And you need to find my green and yellow cup."

Charlie stood and took two steps before Edith cleared her throat.

He turned back and she was pointing at the table. "Aren't you forgetting something?"

Shit. Charlie pulled out a ten dollar bill and dropped it on the table. "I'll see you tomorrow night."

"Don't be late."

Charlie went past Mac, who looked like he was about to say something but stopped himself. He simply waved and Charlie slunk out the back door and down the steps, getting into his beat-up van.

He usually got a coffee to go, but, he'd been in such a rush, he forgot. Instead, he sipped the warm water left in the green and yellow plastic cup in the van.

Passing Friend

"You carry ice?"

Mac looked up from the counter and took a step back. The guy was huge, easily six and a half feet tall and close to three hundred pounds. He was smiling, but his look was anything but friendly.

"Sure, buddy. You want a cup of it?"

The behemoth lifted his right hand. "If all goes as planned, I'll need to ice this hand."

Mac started to speak but the guy held up a finger. "Don't worry. I'm not going to do anything inside your establishment. You have a nice little place here." He glanced out the back door. "I might need you to look away, if I step out into the alley." He grinned at Mac and extended a meaty hand. "I'm Ike, by the way. Pleasure to meet you."

"Mac."

"You see the girl in the corner that came in with me?"

"I assume your daughter?"

Ike grinned. "She's actually an old friend's daughter. I knew Mr. Brown when we served together. He's out near Seattle, but, lo and behold, his little girl got mixed up with an asshole, and they moved to Orange Park. Not too far from here. I did my buddy a solid and pulled her from a bad situation."

"You sound like a good friend," Mac said. "Was it without incident?"

Ike shrugged. "So far. He doesn't even know she's gone yet. I have an hour to kill before I put her ass on a plane in Daytona Beach. I decided to stop and get something to eat and relax for a bit. The poor kid just turned eighteen and she's never even seen the beach."

"Wow."

"Yeah. He kept her inside, and his damn parents helped him to keep her under lock and key. She's been in Florida for four months without seeing anything more than the local Publix. On top of that, the beatings started days after they got here. I can't tolerate some weakling beating on women. She's all of one-twenty wet, and he has about a hundred pounds on her. If he wants to fight, he can come meet me." Ike held up his fist, again.

"I doubt he'll find you, especially if he's in Orange Park. That's an hour away."

Ike grinned. "He's working for a contractor in Palm Coast today, just over the bridge. I'm guessing he'll find out where I am."

"Especially when he calls her and you tell him," Mac said.

"Of course. Can we get two coffees?" Ike looked at the specials board. "What's on the Cowabunga sandwich?"

"Roast beef, pastrami, ham, bacon, red onion, lettuce, tomato and horseradish sauce on a Portuguese roll."

"I'll take two of them." He turned and pointed at the girl. "Ronni, you hungry?"

She shrugged, looking tired.

"How about a fried egg sandwich with six strips of bacon on it? Cheddar cheese, red onion, lettuce and tomato on a bagel of your choice. It's not on the menu but it's one of the best sellers," Mac said. "And it tastes amazing."

"That sounds pretty good. Throw in two of those."

Mac smiled. "Four sandwiches in total?"

"Yep. I'll eat whatever of hers she doesn't eat."

"Have a seat and I'll run you out two coffees. Milk and sugar behind you."

Mac went to work making the coffees, and thanking his lucky stars this giant was hungry and he'd done nothing to cross him.

* * * * *

Ronni fingered her sandwich but had only taken two bites of it. She was staring out the front window and tapping her index finger on her coffee cup.

"You should eat something. You need to finish your sandwich. Are you going to finish your sandwich?"

She absently pushed the red plastic basket across the table to Ike.

He picked it up and took a bite. "Suit yourself."

Ronni glanced down at her cell phone on the table.

"Has douche bag called yet?" he said between bites, knowing the answer. He was acting casual but watching her like a hawk. The first hour was crucial in situations like this. No matter how horrible the guy had been to her, the fear was she would stumble back to him, listen to his lies about being sorry and never doing it again, and everything would be honeymoon wonderful for a few days or weeks. Then it would begin again, and it would keep progressing until she was permanently injured or dead. Ike knew the look on Ronni's face and he didn't like it.

"He hasn't called." She picked up her phone and scrolled through her messages. "It might be awhile before his mom realizes I crawled out the window with my suitcase."

"He'll find out soon enough." Ike finished the fourth sandwich. "By then, you need to be on a plane and halfway to Seattle. I know you think you love this guy, but you're really young. You're a pretty girl."

Ronni scrunched up her nose. "Dude, are you hitting on me?"

"Don't flatter yourself. I like my women a bit more experienced."

"You like old women because you're old?" she said and laughed.

"Funny."

30

"How do you know my dad?"

"I served with your dad. I called him Mister Brown and he called me Mister White."

"Why?"

"Ever see the movie *Reservoir Dogs*?"

"Never heard of it."

"Holy crap. I owe your dad a beating, I think. How could he not let you see it? It's one of the greatest violent movies ever. The bank robbers use aliases. So, a few of us started doing it as a joke."

"Did you rob banks with my dad?"

"Not that I'm aware of." Ike chugged his coffee. "Why, did your dad rob a bank?"

Ronni shrugged. "I have no idea. I haven't seen him since I was two."

"What?"

"I lived with my mom and wasn't allowed to see my dad until I turned eighteen, but then Jeb and I came to Florida."

Ike laughed, a big throaty sound that quieted the café. He didn't care. "Wait a minute. Sixty-two questions just popped into my head with the one sentence you just spit out, so we're going to break it down one thing at a time."

Ronni shrugged and sipped her coffee. "Sure."

"Why didn't you see your dad for so long?"

"My mom and dad got divorced when I was little. I moved to California with her, and she got remarried and had my two brothers. I was told Darryl was my dad, but then I found my birth certificate when I was fifteen. Mom said, when I turned eighteen, I could find my real dad, but Darryl was always a great father to me."

"But you found your real dad?"

"It wasn't hard. It's not like in movies and stuff. I just Googled his name and found out all kinds of things about him. Then I called him and we talked a few times. Mom and Darryl got divorced about a year ago, and I've kept in touch with both dads. I was going to visit him a couple of times before Jeb's family came to Florida. I just never got the chance."

"So, you're getting on this plane and meeting your dad for the first time, really. That's pretty heavy, but such a blessing. Some kids never get a chance to meet their real father or mother. This is a new lease on life for you."

"I suppose so." Ronni glanced at her phone again.

"Now, here's the big question... why the heck would you date a man named Jeb?"

Ronni shrugged. "He was really nice to me at first. He treated me like a princess."

Ike smiled. She didn't get his lame joke. She was right; he was old. "How old is your mom?"

"Old, like you. In her forties."

"Ancient." Ike stood and stretched. "You almost ready to go?"

Ronni shrugged, yet again. To Ike, it seemed her signature move, the uninterested response to most questions. She was dying to hear the phone ring and was ready to listen to his bullshit promises about not hurting her ever again, and his regret over having done so. Now that she was gone from the house, he'd play nice until he got his hands on her.

"We'll head out to Daytona Beach and put you on the plane. But first, I want to walk over to the pier. You interested in seeing the ocean?"

Ronni smiled. "That would be great. I've only ever seen the Pacific."

"It's not much different. Waves and sand and people who have no business being in bikinis. But it's nice and relaxing." Ike went to the counter and tossed down two twenties.

"Let me get your change," Mac said.

"Keep it." Ike handed him another twenty dollar bill. "If all goes as planned, I'll be back around in an hour or so. I might even be hungry again. The sandwiches were killer."

"Listen..." Mac started to say but Ike smiled and put up his fist.

"You won't even know I'm here. Trust me. I only told you to be nice. To be a good neighbor and all that. All I'm asking is for you and your wife to stay inside and not worry about a little noise out back. I won't ruin anything or upset the farmer's market or you and your livelihood." Ike leaned forward. "But I do need to take care of this, and right a wrong."

* * * * *

Ronni took off her sneakers and socks and held them up. "Where can I put these?"

"Just put them off to the side."

32

"What if someone takes them?"

Ike laughed. "No one is crazy enough to touch your things, believe me. They will be safe and sound."

"I'm going to put my feet in the water."

"Knock yourself out."

Ronni looked down at Ike's boots, as he stood on the beach. "Aren't you going to come in?"

"Not today. Go have fun. I see the ocean every day of my life. I live on the water. For you, this is exciting and new. For me, this is home."

"What do you mean you live on the water?"

"I have a boat. As soon as you get on the plane, I get to go back and relax on *Knight's Mare* and worry about dinner. It's a hard life, but someone's gotta live it." Ike pointed at the ocean. "Go play; we only have a few minutes. Give me your purse and phone, too."

Ronni handed everything over to him. Ike palmed her purse and put her cell phone in his pocket.

With a big smile, Ronni ran to the waves and splashed into the surf.

"Don't get too wet; you have to get on my bike," Ike said, but she wasn't listening. She was splashing around, kicking her feet and laughing like she was eight and not eighteen. Ike saw her visibly relax, her shoulders no longer slumping and her face lighting up. She was a good looking kid, and it made him angry to know someone was treating her so badly. This guy deserved a beating.

Ronni was about fifteen feet out, in ankle-deep water, when Ike felt her phone vibrate in his pocket. Still watching her, he pulled it out and cupped it in his beefy hand as he accepted the call, saying nothing.

"Honey? Baby?" The guy on the phone's voice was frantic.

Ike paused for a second and tried not to smile. Ronni was oblivious, getting her feet and the bottom of her shorts wet, as she jogged toward the Flagler Pier.

"Here's the deal, buddy. She's not coming back to you."

Ike could hear the douche bag's voice drop down an octave. "Who is this?"

"You don't need to know that. All you need to know is, she's getting her shit together without you."

"Put her on the phone."

Ike laughed. "I know you did not just give me an order, Jeb."

"I'm warning you..."

"Let me stop you right there, little buddy. You have no idea who you are dealing with, but I'm someone who currently holds all the cards. If I were you, I'd be much nicer. I'd also kiss some ass if you want to ever see her again. Do we have an understanding?"

"Yes."

"I didn't hear you, Jeb."

"Yes... sir."

"Almost good." Ike put the phone near his chest when Ronni looked over at him and smiled. Ike waved and causally turned his back on her, putting the phone back to his ear. "Here's the deal, sport: I'm going to talk to Ronni for a little bit, get her something to eat. Then I'm going to ask her if she wants to see you one last time. To say good bye."

"I don't want her to leave me."

"Well, you should have thought about that, right?"

"Whatever she said was a lie. I swear."

"Look, I'm sure this is just a big misunderstanding. I get it. I was young and in love once. Chicks can be crazy, right? They make you do stupid things you regret. I know what happens."

"Yeah, exactly."

Ike could hear Jeb sounding relieved on the other end of the phone. The chicken-shit thought he had a legitimate chance to sink his claws into her, turn her back around, and never let her go again. "Give me an hour and a half. You know where Kokomo's Café is on Flagler Beach?"

"Is she there?"

"No, Jeb. Listen to what I'm saying to you. I'm going to get her something to eat, somewhere else, before we meet there. But I don't want a scene. Meet us on the back deck behind the restaurant, and come alone. I don't want her scared off if your old man is with you, got it?"

"Sure, sure."

"Remember, just you."

"You got it. Thanks."

Ike smiled. "No, Jeb, you can thank me later."

* * * * *

The ride back to Flagler Beach from Daytona Beach was beautiful, and Ike enjoyed the ride as he cruised on his Harley. Initially, he thought about seeing what Brewski was doing, but decided he'd handle this on his own. Ike hoped Jeb brought his old man with him, and whoever else wanted an ass kicking.

Ike parked in front of Kokomo's and went around the corner, coming up just as a skinny punk kid and three buddies, one of them clearly his father, stepped out from the alley near the café. They were all looking around.

"Hang out near the park so we don't scare her," Jeb was saying. He turned to his old man. "Why don't you go inside and grab me a coffee? Then, when you see this scumbag, you can help me kick his ass and drag her to the car before the cops come."

Despite his size, Ike was invisible until he stopped right in front of the group and clapped his hands. They all jumped.

"Can we help you?" Jeb asked, taking a step back.

Ike could see there was a baseball bat leaning against the fence, within reach of the punk.

"Maybe." Ike leaned forward and squinted at Jeb's face.

"What the fuck are you doing?"

"I'm wondering if your nose has ever been broken."

The kid looked confused. "No."

Ike put up his fist. "You mean, not yet."

Jeb's father stepped up and threw a haymaker, which Ike blocked easily. He slammed the man in the face with an open palm.

"Shit, I didn't have time to see if your daddy's nose had ever been broken." Ike clapped again. "But I can definitely see it is now."

"Get him," Jeb growled to his friends. They didn't move.

"I have no beef with you guys. Your buddy Jeb here thinks beating a little girl is macho, but I have to disagree. In fact, it is my goal to beat him to within an inch of his life. If you are stupid enough to get in my way, I will have no choice but to hurt you. Seriously hurt you. Do you want to take a beating, and perhaps a broken limb or two, for this scumbag and his daddy? Woman beating punk needs to get his ass kicked."

One of the guys looked at Jeb and put his hands up. "I didn't know you were beating her, dude. Not cool." He turned to Ike. "Can we leave?"

Ike waved them off, just as Jeb's dad got up on one knee, his face a bloody mess."

"Can we talk about this first?" Jeb asked. "She's a real bitch."

"No woman deserves to get hit. I would wonder why you weren't taught this as a kid, but it's obvious your old man has no common sense. I'm sure you grew up watching this jerkoff slapping your mom around. For that, I'm going to break one of his limbs."

Jeb grabbed the baseball bat and swung it, connecting with Ike's extended forearm. Jeb dropped the bat when it vibrated off the tree limb of Ike, who smiled.

"If that leaves a bruise, I'm going to come back and hurt you even more than I'm going to hurt you now. Understand?"

Jeb put his hands in front of his face and slumped down against the fence, curling up.

Ike kicked the dad in the stomach as he tried to rise, putting him back down. He turned to Jeb. "Are you crying?"

"I'm sorry."

"Oh, it's too late for all that. You came here, not to apologize, but to beat her so bad she'd be too afraid to leave you. Now, I'm going to beat you so bad you'll never want to hear her name. Stand up and take it like a man."

Jeb didn't move.

Ike grabbed Jeb by the hair and helped him to his feet. "I'm going to start by breaking your nose."

It's All About Time

Reba Port wanted to lift her laptop and slam it to the floor, before stepping on it, kicking it across the small room and breaking it into tiny little pieces.

Her twins were home and, currently, arguing over the game controllers, even though they each had their own. Reba's husband, Sam, owned his own software business and worked from the extra bedroom upstairs. From 9 am until 5 pm, except for a regimented lunch hour from noon until 1 pm, his door was closed and he was working. He was the bread winner, but she wanted to be the famous writer and turn this hobby into a viable income, one she could be proud of. She wanted a steady income so she would be seen as more than Sam's doting wife and mother to the twins. She wanted her own career, her own money, and she wanted to do it in style.

This book was her ticket to this and more. Only, right now, she couldn't string three words together to form a sentence without freaking out. She felt like a wannabe hack. Who was going to read her lame story about a little boy who saw ghosts in his house?

Reba was glad no one else was in the side room of Kokomo's Café with her, because she probably looked insane. She took turns covering her face with her hands and then shaking them at the computer screen she felt was mocking her.

She knew how the story would end, and the first six chapters were brilliant. Her mother, back home in Illinois, had read and loved it, so far. She had asked a few questions, so Reba knew she'd actually taken the time to read it. The middle chapters, however, weren't coming to her. She needed to move the character along and get him to see the ghost his mom couldn't see but could hear.

But how? Reba shadow-punched the laptop in frustration. She giggled, suddenly, when she thought of the faces Mac and Ginny would give her if she started screaming, or what they'd do if she smashed the side window out with her computer. "Probably call the police," she whispered. She was losing her mind. Reba decided to check her e-mail, Facebook, Twitter, Pinterest, Instagram and LinkedIn accounts, quickly, before writing again. Maybe she could find inspiration among the cat memes and one-sided religious and political rants.

Reba didn't know how much time she'd wasted until her cell phone rang. She checked the time: 12:25. *Time flies when you're wasting time*, she thought. She was going to write that down as soon as she answered the phone. She was sure she could use the line in this book. "Hello?"

"Hey... where are you?"

"I'm at Kokomo's Café, writing. I told you this morning I was going to catch up on my book."

"How's it going?" Sam asked.

Reba stared at her computer, with an angry cat meme staring at her. "Great," she mumbled. "How's work for you, today?"

"It's going great. Just hanging around here... getting hungry."

"I'm a bit hungry, too."

"What are you bringing home?" her husband asked.

Ah, he's waiting for me to give him lunch, she thought. "I'm not coming home just yet. I want to finish this chapter." *I really just want to write a damn sentence without wanting to kill someone.*

"Alright..." Sam paused on the phone.

"I have work to do," Reba finally said.

"I'm hungry," he blurted.

"Then make something. You're a grown man. I think one lunch by yourself won't kill you."

"The twins are hungry, too. There's nothing to eat in the house. Why can't you get us McDonald's?"

Reba sighed. "I'm not driving over the bridge to get you burgers when you can make a sandwich. There's ham, salami and cheese. Bread is on the counter. That shouldn't be hard to do."

"I guess. I lost half of my lunch break."

Reba laughed. "You work at home. I don't think the internet will crash if you get back online at 1:08. I'll be home when I get home."

"What's for dinner?"

Reba wished she was home, so she could slam the laptop over Sam's head and kill two birds with one stone. Finally, she took a deep breath and calmed down. "I'll bring home McDonald's for dinner."

* * * * *

The creepy guy was sitting in the corner again. Reba smiled at him but he put his head down, the laptop suddenly the most important thing in the world.

"What's his deal?" Reba asked Mac when she went to the counter to order a chicken salad sandwich. All the talk of food with Sam had gotten her hungry, and she figured a break from writing (alright, she'd thought about writing) would do her good. Then, she would jump into it and catch up.

"Who?"

Reba leaned in and dropped her voice to a conspiratorial whisper. "The big guy in the corner with the crazy goatee. I see him every time I come in."

"He comes in at our opening and he'll be here until we close. He rarely talks to anyone, always eats lunch alone, and always orders the same thing: tuna on a cinnamon raisin bagel. He dinks three cups of coffee, and he tips well. I think he's a writer."

"Really?" Now she was interested. Maybe she could pick his brain, see what his secrets were. A fellow traveler on the road to writing. How fun. "I might go and introduce myself."

"Good luck. He rarely speaks or looks up from his computer. Sometimes Ginny and I will say weird things when he's the only one around, and he doesn't even hear us."

"He probably does, and puts it into his story. I wonder what he writes. He's scary-looking. He probably writes about serial killers."

"Someone said he writes about zombies," Ginny said, as she came around the counter. "I don't even know his name."

"Next time he pays with a credit card, you'll see the name."

"Nope. He always pays in cash. He has the laptop, usually facing him, and unless you climb up to the window over his head, who knows what he's doing for nine hours a day." Mac went into the kitchen to make her lunch.

"Go say hi," Ginny said.

"Would you?"

"If I were you? Yes."

"What if you were Ginny?"

"Not a chance. But that's just me. I've tried to engage him in conversation on slow days but he grunts and never makes eye contact. He's harmless; he's just really shy."

"Or he's trying to figure out what your skin will look like as a mask." Reba was fascinated by the many possible scenarios going through her head, most of them about this guy doing indescribable things to flesh.

Ginny shrugged. "Either way, he's a steady customer and he tips well. It's nice to have some regulars, and, on the rare occasion he isn't here right at eight or skips a day, there are quite a few people who notice. I think it's fun, and he's harmless."

Reba stared at him, again. "They always say that on the news about the next door neighbor, who snapped and killed his entire family."

"You're morbid, today," Ginny said.

"I write about ghosts. I need to stay focused." Reba's ideas were coming at her at full speed right now, and she decided to sit in the main room, keep this creepy guy within sight for inspiration, and write until it was time to go home.

* * * * *

Creepy Guy (she's decided she wasn't going to disturb him) was staring at Reba. She put her face back down and tried to concentrate on her laptop. *In all fairness, I've been staring at him for the last hour*, she thought. *He keeps catching me doing it.*

She was seated at the table straight in front of the main door, her head casually cranked to her left so she could watch him. Creepy Guy was writing something, but he did the peck and poke method with his two meaty index fingers, eyes watching his digits as he typed. He was pretty fast, his eyes glued to the screen except when he caught her staring. He didn't give her a mean look. It was more... indifferent? He was in his own little world. He'd look up when new customers came in or old ones left, but he never made eye contact, never said a word to anyone, and looked away when people gave him a nod or hello.

40

The window above his head was too high for her, and she knew, outside, there was nothing for her to stand on to see what he was writing. With her luck, Reba figured she'd fall and break her leg or arm and have to explain to the police what she was doing scaling the building. It wasn't that high… Reba went out the front door, leaving her laptop and bag behind. The front deck ended at the side of the building, a four-foot rail jutting out. She leaned against it. The window was farther away than she thought.

Reba looked around. There was no one right around her, but the farmer's market was still going. Although, by this point, some of them had either sold out or packed it up and decided to call it a day. She pulled the plastic chair to the rail and stood on it, getting a leg onto the rail. She was a small woman but afraid of heights, and, even only ten feet off the ground, she could feel her knees shaking.

She balanced against the building and got both feet on the rail, squatting and facing the park. But, now, she realized she was facing the wrong way. She'd need to turn around and lean as far to her right as she could. If she was lucky, she'd be tall enough and able to grab the windowsill, before gravity pulled her over the edge, where she'd land on the hood of her own mini-van.

A woman across the street was looking at watermelons and her young daughter was staring at Reba.

"Holy crap," Reba thought and almost fell off the rail. She stepped down in shame and sat down in the chair.

"What are you doing?"

Reba looked up to see Bettie, the woman who lived upstairs over Kokomo's Café. With her wild white hair, big smile and hippy fashion sense, she was quite unique, even in a town known for its characters.

Bettie pointed at the rail and put a huge smile on her face. "Are you trying to climb the building?"

"I was trying to look in the window."

"There are easier windows to access, you know."

Reba laughed. "I'm trying to look in and see what the guy in the corner is writing."

"Why?" Bettie asked and sat down next to Reba. She leaned over, conspiratorially. "Do you think he's doing something illegal? Maybe he's planning to rob the place. He's casing the joint."

"You have quite the imagination. You should have been a writer," Reba said.

Bettie nodded her head. "Someday. If I only had the time. Instead, I spend my days going to the gym, riding my bike and living a clean life." She threw her hands up in the air. "Who better than me to breathe this wonderful air and see these amazing sights, right? It's a dirty job, but somebody's gotta do it. Might as well be me."

"True." Reba stood. "I need to get back inside and actually get some writing done."

"Good luck. I'm already late for paddleboard meditation. It's so nice out on the water. I'll be back around later; maybe I'll see you."

* * * * *

Reba searched through her Facebook friends and their friends, trying to find a profile picture that matched the Creepy Guy. Everyone was on Facebook these days. She hoped he didn't have a stupid picture of his cat as his profile, or some lame meme about zombies. If he wrote about zombies, maybe it would be a cover to one of his books.

He's not very good at promoting, she thought. *If he was, he'd let everyone know his name and have a pile of books at the table for people to buy.*

When her book was finished and published, she'd carry a stack of bookmarks around in her purse and bag, and hand them to anyone who even glanced at her. She figured she'd be doing the local television and radio circuit, so people would see her face and hear her voice and know who she was. Reba thought about the fun of being out to dinner with Sam and the twins and random strangers stopping by her table and asking for an autograph and picture.

Too bad Oprah isn't still doing the book club, Reba thought. She was sure this book (when finished) would be a perfect addition, because it was a YA story but dealt with adult issues the parents could also enjoy.

"How's the writing coming?" Mac asked, as he went past her and dropped off two food baskets to the older man and the brunette sitting with him.

"Oh, it's… coming," Reba said but when she looked down at the screen it was mocking her, the cursor blinking at the same spot it was sitting when she got here. She'd been so preoccupied with

Creepy Guy, her work had suffered. "I need to get through this chapter."

Mac grinned and went back behind the counter.

Reba needed to ignore Creepy Guy, so she looked at the old man and the woman he was with. The guy was her dad. It wasn't a guess. Reba had just overheard her call him dad. She guessed, by the way they were dressed (he had on a hideous Hawaiian shirt and mismatched shorts, topped off with a new straw hat, and she had on a one-piece, black bathing suit with a white, thin shirt and shorts set covering her ample figure), they were tourists, here to soak up the Florida sun. Due to their pale complexions, she imagined they were from the northern part of the country or maybe even Canadians, but they lacked the accents.

His daughter was pretty but very plain, with only a hint of makeup. She was covering up her body and, while she wasn't fat, she could stand to lose a few pounds. *Plump*, Reba thought. *She's a chunky bottle blonde, with her darker roots showing. On vacation with her dad because se doesn't have a boyfriend and isn't comfortable with her own body. What a shame.*

Reba wasn't being judgmental. She was looking at them, with her trained writer's eye, formulating a back-story for the two of them. She collected these pieces in her head and could pull them out at will, as long as she remembered them. Someday, all of these scenes would be written and sold, and she'd earn a living on these keen observations.

The dad is dying, and his last wish is to see the Atlantic Ocean, it hit her. *In Montreal, he never got to see the water.* Reba made a mental note to see how close Montreal was to the ocean. She imagined something sad and drawn out to tug at the sympathy strings. Maybe some new Canadian disease, or maybe the daughter (she would name her Amber) was on a business trip to Saigon or Brazil and contracted a rare virus, capable of killing people or making them insane with rage, and then they'd start biting everyone and spreading the disease and…

Reba looked back over at Creepy Guy, who was two-finger typing like a madman. What was he writing? Hours and hours, this dude was working on something. If he was a writer, he had to be prolific. He might have seventy books out for all she knew. Maybe he was really famous and the gray goatee and bald head was a disguise. What if he was a famous actor, hanging around the café and rewriting his next blockbuster? Reba squinted. She tried to picture him with hair and maybe twenty pounds lighter (actors took on and lost weight at will), and he did have arresting eyes, like… Matthew McConaughey, maybe? Nah. Sam Elliot with the eyes.

Her phone rang and she stumbled to answer before it rang again. Creepy Guy was looking at her and so were Amber and her dying dad. It was Sam.

"Exactly when are you coming home?" he asked, as sweetly as she knew he could.

"Soon. I am almost done with this chapter." Reba wanted to smash the laptop again, anger welling up. "Didn't you have lunch?"

"Yes. Hours ago. It's almost five. Are you going to get McDonald's?"

"Of course. I'll be home in twenty minutes."

"No rush," Sam said. She knew what that meant: the twins were driving him nuts, and they were hungry. It must be bad, since she looked at her watch and it was only 4:42. He never came out of his office before five, if he could help it.

Reba began packing her things, hoping tomorrow or, maybe, late tonight, she could catch up. She had an epic YA ghost story in her head and it wasn't going to write itself.

Some Of Your Love

Her dad poked the top of his sandwich and smiled. "Authentic beach food."

Darlene laughed. "I'm guessing you can get a pastrami sandwich back home in Maine, too."

"Not like this," he said. He took a big bite from it, flecks of provolone and Granddaddy's Mustard on his creased chin. He shook the sandwich at Darlene. "This is the real deal." He grinned and took another bite.

Her turkey club panini was amazing, Darlene had to admit. Turkey, bacon and cheddar and herb mayo. She had asked for extra lettuce, tomato but no onion. She hated onion. Even though she was twenty-eight years old, her dad would still order them pizza with onions on it and then act indignant when she explained/screamed, for the millionth time, onions were gross. Darlene thought he did it on purpose, instead of just ordering half the pie with extra onions. He got hers every time.

This vacation was her idea, because he wasn't getting any younger and she wasn't going to meet the man of her dreams and take a cruise anytime soon. Besides, she liked the company of her dad. "I like Flagler Beach. Where'd you hear about this place?"

"When I worked for Saco Defense, I used to call down to Pensacola and order parts for the Desert Eagle." Her dad had been a foreman for the company in Saco, Maine, during their brief tenure manufacturing the large frame semi-auto pistol. Darlene was the proud owner of a Desert Eagle made by her dad. "This guy I would talk to all the time, he was a funny guy. Close to retirement. He lived his entire life in Florida, and we'd talk about the weather, as you can imagine. He'd bust my balls about how cold it was in Maine and I'd laugh at him when it hit triple digits. A great guy."

"Dad, you still didn't answer the question."

"What was it?" he asked between bites, but she could see he was messing with her, as usual. "Why we came here?"

"Forget it." Darlene wasn't going to take the bait. "I'm just going to enjoy my vacation and not make fun of the silly outfit you are wearing."

"This is called Tourist Chic."

"I don't think so. You look ridiculous." Darlene apprized her dad's choice of wardrobe for today: gaudy Hawaiian shirt, big straw hat he'd purchased for too much money when they were in Daytona Beach yesterday, and shorts that might be green or maybe teal, but they were so busy her eyes hurt looking at them. Of course, the old man still had on his black tube socks and 1920's era tennis shoes. She took another bite of her sandwich and saw he'd gone back to his with lust in his eyes. "Fine, I'll ask: how did you find this particular beach town?"

"Murph told me about it. He'd been here with his wife before she passed, and his kid. They had vacationed here once or twice, back when this was nothing more than a wooden pier and some summer homes. He said the bridge was this tiny little thing spanning the river. He must have talked about it a dozen times over the months."

"You talked to him quite a bit."

Her dad shrugged his shoulders. "I knew the end was coming for the factory, and I just wanted to bide my time. I knew I'd be back in Dexter making shoes soon enough, and it was fine with me. I didn't have to pay for these long distance phone calls, either. Murph knew we'd all be out of business soon enough, and he was right. Two weeks after Saco closed its doors for good, the company he worked for did the same. Without our big contract, they were ruined. Such is life." He popped the last bite of sandwich into his mouth and smiled. "They don't make them like that in Maine."

"It must be the water." Darlene checked her watch. They'd wandered around for most of the morning and afternoon, killing time in and out of the little shops dotting the beach. "I'm glad you met him on the phone. Maybe you can look him up while we're in Florida?"

Her dad waved his hand. "Nah. He's probably dead by now. Heck, he's even older than me. He said this place was several hours drive for him. I never got his phone number; it's not like we were dating."

"I'm sure you asked and he said he wasn't attracted to you."

Her dad wrinkled his nose at her and frowned. "Not funny."

Darlene had to laugh. "Sorry, I keep forgetting how manly you are. So old school. You can't even joke around about another man, lest I think my dad is gay."

He looked uncomfortable and she loved hitting this playful nerve with him. She decided to cut him some slack, since they were on vacation and having a few good days.

"Where are we eating tonight?" she asked him.

"Around here would be nice. We should ask a local what they suggest."

Darlene looked around. There was a big guy at the next table but his face was buried in his laptop. The woman on the other side of them was staring at the big guy in the corner, which was creepy. Maybe they knew each other? "I'll go ask the people who work here."

The back door opened and a man and woman entered, both laughing and sharing a joke. Darlene stopped when they walked to the counter, but the man turned and smiled at her. "Please, after you. We have no idea what we want."

Darlene stared at him. He was gorgeous, with beautiful blue eyes, a nice physique and such a great smile. His face was so... right. He was matinee idol handsome, and he had such a presence, to her. She'd never encountered a man like this before.

"Hello?" the woman with him said, impatiently. She put her hand on the counter. "Since she's not responding, can I get a Tazo Chai tea. John, what do you want?"

He was staring at Darlene and smiling, nodding his head slightly. Darlene knew the feeling was mutual.

The other woman grabbed him by the arm and swung him around. "John Murphy, I'm talking to you."

* * * * *

"What did they say?"

"Who?" Darlene sat back down and felt like she was underwater.

Her dad pointed, at the counter, with a laugh. "You went up to ask for a great local spot to eat. What did you do, forget why you went up?"

"Yeah, I guess I did. I got distracted."

"Then go ask."

Darlene looked at the couple, who were now seated across from the counter and waiting for their order. She didn't want to walk and stand with her back to them. Her ass was fat, even covered in this outfit. She was pudgy and unattractive, and this guy's girlfriend or wife was very attractive... and skinny. This guy (John Murphy, she'd never forget his name) was into small women, not bloated monsters like her. Ugh, she hated herself right now. Why was she beating herself up over some guy she didn't know? He was with someone. She was with her dad.

"Fine, you'll make me go up. I'm an old man. I hope I don't throw out my hip walking up so we can plan our next meal. You're a control freak like your mom, you know that? But don't worry about me or my bad leg or my dementia."

"You don't have a bad leg. You are demented, though. I'm going. Who's the control freak?" Darlene got up.

"Who always gets his way?"

Darlene decided to order something else to drink. "You want iced tea or a smoothie?"

"A beer would be perfect."

"Iced tea it is." Darlene went back to the counter, blushing when John looked at her and smiled. She put her back to him and wanted to die. The woman behind the counter was in the kitchen talking to her husband, and Darlene tapped the counter, impatiently, to get her attention. She wanted to get back to her chair and cover her ass as quickly as possible.

"Are your sandwiches good?" Ginny asked.

"Yes, perfect. Can I get two iced teas?"

"No sugar?"

Darlene was confused. She hadn't ordered iced tea with no sugar.

She heard John laugh behind her. "The lady would like two sweet teas."

Ginny grinned. "I thought so. I'm just teasing you. People from up North always wonder what I'm talking about. I enjoy the game."

Darlene half-turned, awkwardly, toward John, who met her gaze and smiled. "Thank you."

"No problem." John nodded to her, before he frowned. His wife or girlfriend was clearly making faces at him. "What? Just being friendly," he whispered. "Relax."

"Two sweet teas," Darlene said, still looking at John and the back of his girl's head. Wow, was she a bitch. If he was her man, she'd treat him right. How could you not smile when he smiled? He seemed so comforting and nice. She was sure his jokes were hysterical, and she envisioned nights spent drinking too much wine, sitting on his yacht and watching the sun dip into the ocean, and feeding him strawberries dipped in chocolate...

Damn, get your shit together, she thought. Who even said he was rich? Darlene was getting herself worked up and she didn't like it. He was with someone, he was beautiful, and he had no interest in her. He was probably being nice because he felt sorry for her. *Honey, I'm being nice to the fat chick because she's probably still a virgin and she'll never kiss a man*, Darlene thought he was thinking. *Why would I want Darlene Bobich when I have a skinny, little, stuck-up, snobby bitch like you as my arm-trophy?*

Darlene noticed the couple had wedding rings and wanted to kick herself. It was even worse than she thought.

She was about to walk back to the table with the two sweet teas when she realized the actual reason - again - she was up here. "Excuse me. Can you suggest a good place to eat tonight for dinner?"

"What are you looking for?"

Darlene didn't know off-hand. "Something good, I guess. My dad has this idea everything he eats in Florida needs to be authentic Florida food. He's goofy. He loved the pastrami sandwich, though."

"It was authentically made in this kitchen," Mac said from the back. "Does he like seafood?"

"Yes."

Ginny glanced at Mac and nodded. "You can't beat the Golden Lion. They have a fish and chips special that's been winning awards for over fifteen years. You can sit upstairs and look out at the ocean."

"Sounds perfect," Darlene said. "Where is it?"

"North 5th Street and A1A. You can't miss it."

"That sounds like a great place. I was going to ask you the best place for seafood," John said.

Darlene fought to turn and look at him. Was he mocking her now? She wanted to turn at him and toss the iced tea - fuck, sweet tea! - in his damn face. Instead, she thanked the owner and went back to the table. He was a married douche bag.

*   *   *   *   *

"Maybe you'll get lucky and find yourself a man," her dad said, as he stuffed Lay's barbeque chips into his mouth. "Stranger things have happened."

"Sometimes you make it very hard to love you."

He shrugged. "Your mom used to say that, too. Hell, she got cancer just to get away from me."

"I told you to stop saying that; it isn't funny."

"She'll meet me at the Pearly Gates and tell Saint Peter not to let me in, just so she can see me squirm one last time. She had a wicked pissa sense of humor, that woman. God knows I loved her, but she deserved a pop in the kisser every now and then. The only thing that stopped me was her left hook. The woman could go toe to toe with Ali."

"I hope I go before you, too. I'm going to stand, hand in hand, with her."

"You forget: I have a ton of friends already up there, and I've been adding them to my nightly prayers. They'll counter your protest, and Saint Peter will likely carry me in, himself. You can't stop me."

Darlene was about to comment when she saw John and his wife get up from their table and exit through the back door, but not before John (holding the door for his skinny-bitch wife) looked back at her and, definitely, smiled.

"Why are men such dirt-bags?" she asked out loud.

"All men in general, or is there a special one in your life? Why haven't I met this guy yet?"

"Forget it, dad." Darlene felt foolish. She'd spent her lunch obsessing over some guy who obviously cheated on his wife, or was mocking the fat girl because he had money or was a megalomaniac. She just wanted to go back to Maine and go back to work behind the makeup counter, hang out with her friends, and spend the rest of her life not looking back on this jerk.

John Murphy. Damn you.

"You know, if you told me you were a lesbian, I'd still love you," her dad said.

Darlene laughed. "God, you are such an idiot. I love you."

"I love you, my lesbian daughter."

"I'm into dudes. Sorry to disappoint you. I'm sure you'd be the cool old guy with the lesbian kid at the VFW. You can talk to the other men about how hip a parent you are, and then tell them about when I was six and I cried when I didn't get a G.I. Joe for Christmas."

"You didn't do that."

"And I'm not a lesbian. I'm just... unlucky with men."

"Someday, you'll find the man of your dreams and you're breath will catch in your throat and you'll forget about everything else. Like I did when I saw your mom at the dance in Bangor. Holding hands with Bruce Fairchild. Bastard. But I broke them up, and, last I heard, Bruce owns a bunch of shrimp boats in Canada. He might have gotten the money, but I got the girl."

Darlene looked at the closed back door of Kokomo's Café. "What do I do if I find him and he's already taken?"

"You fight for him."

"What if he's already married?" she asked, turning to her dad.

He laughed. "You pray to God that guy's wife is really as big a bitch as you think she is, and he comes to his senses. Something tells me they'll be at the Golden Lion tonight. You might want to get cleaned up."

"I'm not taking you dressed like that, old man."

He took the straw hat off and looked at it. "I look good in this." He put it back on and winked at his daughter.

And Your Dreams Come True

Ginny smiled when Danny Street came in. The boy was handsome, and had gone to Flagler Palm Coast High School, with their daughter. He was an amazing guitarist, and, on several Friday nights, had played in the courtyard between Kokomo's Café and Bahama Mama's. Danny drew not only a younger crowd of smiling females, but a mature crowd who loved his acoustic renditions of classic 60's rock and country staples from before he was born.

"I haven't seen you in forever," she said, from behind the counter. "The last thing I heard, you'd gone off to Nashville to become a star."

Danny laughed and tucked his long blond locks behind an ear. "I wish. I went up there to record a few demo tracks, but nothing really came of it." He looked around at the few customers in the main room and leaned forward. "But I have a meeting with a manager today."

Ginny clapped. "Amazing! I knew you'd get somewhere, didn't I always tell you that?"

Mac came out from the kitchen. "Hey, buddy. What's this I hear about you getting rich and famous and forgetting about us little people?"

"You know it will never happen." Danny, again, tucked his long blond hair behind his ear. "I'm going to meet him here later today. I invited the gang to come down so I could talk to them beforehand."

"Taking the whole band with you to Nashville?" Ginny asked.

Danny put his hands up and smiled. "Who can really say? I sure hope so."

"You've jammed with your friends for years and years. How amazing would it be, not only for you to get rich and famous, but to be able to take care of the people around you? They must be excited. Do you want some coffees?"

"I could really use a slice of the six-layer carrot cake. The manager will be here in a couple of hours, so just put it on his tab. He's good for it. Maybe a smoothie, too. I need to focus and relax a bit. I'm going to chill in the side room until the guys get here. It's so great to see you two again."

* * * * *

"Wade, this is difficult, trust me," Danny said.

"Bullshit. I can't believe, after all we've been through, you're going to drop us like this. For what? Some hotshot manager who's going to make you into a star?"

"It does sound kinda cool," Jayce said.

Wade turned to Jayce, who had his sunglasses on despite the fact they were sitting in the side room of Kokomo's Café with the lights off and only natural sunlight peeking through the curtains. "Shut up, you burnout hippie. You always agree with whatever he says, no matter what. Dude, he's dumping us so he can go off and be a star. We're being left behind, don't you get it?"

Jayce shrugged. "I'm happy for him. He's my bro."

Wade turned back to Danny. "We had a deal."

Danny shook his head. "We had a few big dreams, sitting in your mom's garage and jamming, that's all. Look, I'm sorry you're mad. I get it, I do… but this is my chance to make something of myself. You think I want to be trapped in Flagler Beach, playing shitty free shows to mindless tourists? Shit, I'm too good for that."

"What about us?"

Danny sat back and sipped his smoothie. "What about you?"

"I can't believe you're just going to drop us." Wade sat back. "We all had this dream and we all took it seriously."

"Really? Where's Walt?"

"He had to work in his mom's store," Jayce offered. "I need to get back to work soon, too."

Wade pointed at Jayce. "He'll be waiting tables at Java Joint until the day he dies, and he's only twenty two."

Jayce smiled. "I hope so. I love working there."

"That's not the point," Wade said, disgustedly. "Shut up."

54

"What is your point? I have a big meeting soon, and wanted to get this out of the way," Danny said and lifted his fork to take another bite of carrot cake. "When I play the arena in Orlando or maybe the stadium in Jacksonville, you guys will be there. You can hang backstage and I'll introduce you to someone in the business. Maybe, once I get this going, I can sign you to a contract. You could be on my vanity label someday. How cool would that be?"

"Cool," Jayce said.

"Not cool at all," Wade said. "We started out as a heavy metal band. Now you're some cheesy country singer. You don't even own a cowboy hat, and you weren't born on a farm. Shit, you hate country music."

"Some of it is alright," Danny said and took a bite of carrot cake. "I'm learning to like it, and the writers in Nashville are amazing. You have to hear some of the demo stuff I just did. These songs have such hooks."

Wade folded his arms across his chest. "Wow, you aren't even going to write your own songs now. You are beyond a sellout. What about all the metal riffs you wrote? What about a song like "Be With Me" and shit like that? I can see what you used to do here on a Friday night, playing Beach Boys songs for the tourists and making a few bucks. That shit, I got. But this…"

Danny ate another piece of cake. "I recorded two of my own songs, as well."

"Which ones?" Wade asked, knowing he wasn't going to like the answer. Danny had written about half of their band's songs. Even though they were very heavy metal, he knew they could be changed enough. Tune up a guitar, slow the tempo, add more harmonies, and you had a shitty country song.

"I did cool versions of "Be With Me" and "I'm Waiting For The Day" and that's what got me the meeting with a big-shot manager."

Now Wade was pissed. He jumped from his chair. "You can't record "I'm Waiting For The Day" because it's my damn song. I wrote it. All the music is mine, you wrote some of the lyrics last-minute."

Danny shrugged. "According to the publishing, all of the songs are now D Street Music owned and copyrighted. You never filled out paperwork for any of them, and I have all the four-track recordings in my possession. I own them. I didn't want to do this, but I needed something good to bring with me to the table."

Wade was stunned. "Wait… you stole all the songs?"

"No, I copyrighted them. Without it, those songs would never be recorded, except on a crappy four-track machine from the eighties your dad gave us. This way, you'll be able to hear your songs on the radio."

"And know that someone I thought was my best friend and a brother to me is making money off songs I wrote. Most of them were written by me. You can't do this."

"Why are you taking this personal? Eventually, like around my fourth or fifth album, I'll need more songs. Then I can hire you and you'll get some real money. You aren't going to get rich as a cook at Johnny D's. Just relax and see what a good thing this is going to be for all of us."

"My name is nowhere on the copyright?"

"Just mine. I needed to get these legal as quickly as possible."

"Then no one will even know I wrote these songs."

"Co-wrote," Danny said.

Wade clenched his fists. He wanted nothing more than to punch his friend (former friend now) in the face, but knew he'd need to remain as calm as he could and try to convince Danny what he'd done was wrong. "Most of the songs were written by me. Completely. You didn't add a single word to them, and not a note. How is that co-writing?"

"It's not," Danny said and Wade detected a slight smile play across his face. "I own the songs right now, but I will make this better in the future. We've been friends for a long time. I get it. Right now, you might be pissed, but someday we'll look back at this and laugh. The money will start rolling in, and I can put you on my payroll and take care of you. Like as a roadie or guitar tech."

"I'd be a guitar tech," Jayce said and played air guitar.

"I already have one." Danny sipped his smoothie. "But, if I don't think he can handle the job, I'll have my management team get in touch with you for an application."

"Sweet."

"Sweet?" Wade turned to Jayce. "Dude, he just blew you off. He just stole all of our songs, and all of our hard work. He sold out and we got screwed." He turned back to Danny. "I'm going to get a lawyer and I'm going to sue you, you little bastard."

Danny shrugged and sipped his smoothie. "I was hoping it didn't come down to this. Suit yourself. You won't get a dime from me and you'll just look like a fool who wasn't good enough to hang in the spotlight with me. Ever hear of Pete Best?"

"Paul McCartney didn't steal all his songs and then dump him, asshole."

"When I meet with my new manager today, I will make sure he takes care of you. I promise. I know this seems like a bad deal now, but look at it long-term. I can start talking you up in Nashville and Los Angeles and wherever else I go, and tell them I worked with this hot-shit writer. They'll be calling you in no time. Just let me do this my way, or we're all screwed."

Wade pulled his fist back to punch the sonofabitch in the mouth.

Danny put his hands up, still holding the smoothie. "Dude, I swear, if you hit me, I will never mention you at all. You will be nobody. I will help you. Trust me."

Wade wanted to slam his former friend around the room, imagining his blood on the tables and walls. But what would it accomplish? He knew he was going to be screwed over... but what if, there was just a small chance it was true, Danny wasn't lying? What if he really was going to help Wade break into the music business and fulfill the dream they'd all shared since grade school?

"Man, I gotta go to work." Jayce stood up and smiled. "Let me know when you need a new guitar tech or a bassist for your band. Good luck."

Danny smiled. "You, too. I'll come down and see you at Java Joint next time I'm in town. We'll hang and party."

"Sounds cool." Jayce walked out.

"I can't believe you did this," Wade said, before lowering his fists and leaving, as well.

* * * * *

"Stop! You're embarrassing me," Danny said as he leaned on the counter. He made sure to give the masseuse a big grin and show off his dimples, which the older women loved.

"You'll see. I'm so proud of you," Ginny said.

The masseuse put a delicate hand out. "I'm Rene. Pleased to meet you. Your life sounds exciting right now. Congratulations," she said and gave him a big smile.

Danny took her hand and shook it, lightly. She was pretty, probably in her mid- to late-thirties, tanned and blonde. He tried not to stare at her tattoo but failed.

Rene laughed. "It's my pride and joy." The tattoo was a series of vines creeping up her left thigh, starting at the top of her foot. She traced it up her leg and the side of her torso, touching the back of her neck. "All the way up."

"Wow. Did it hurt?"

"It was unbelievable. This half took over six hours," she said and pointed from her foot to her waist. "My body went into shock at the end and we had to stop."

"Crazy. Why would you go back and finish it?"

"I wanted to get it done in one night, but I had to wait a week until the bottom part healed. The next week it took seven hours to finish it. I keep adding little things like butterflies and frogs to it."

"You are an amazing woman," Danny said to her.

Rene grinned. "Thank you. Have a great day." She took her coffee and went out the front door.

Danny casually followed her out and called to her as she was going down the front path. "Rene? Got a second?"

"Sure," she said and stopped. "I'm running a bit late. What's up?"

"I'm wondering what you're doing tonight. My new manager is coming down from New York to sign me to a huge contract, and then we'll probably hit the town and celebrate. It would be nice to have a pretty lady on my arm."

Rene laughed, her eyes sparkling. "I am flattered by the offer, but I'll have to decline. Good luck with everything, Danny."

Danny couldn't believe she was blowing him off. Rene turned and walked to her car. Danny stared at her ass and wanted to see the rest of the tattoo. "Are you serious?"

"Huh?" she said, looking confused, as she put her key in her car   lock.
"I'm offering you the greatest night of your life and you're acting like you're not interested."

Rene opened her car door. "You seem like a nice kid. I'm sure you're a lot of fun, but I'm about ten years older than you and I'm seeing someone. Have a great night."

"You're not all that," Danny stammered. "I can get better than you, and I will. Rooms full of whores."

Rene gave him the finger. "I'm not a whore, little boy. If I were you, I'd go back inside before I step back around this car and kick your ass."

Danny waved her off and went back inside. *What an idiot she was anyway*, he thought. She wasn't worth his time, even if she was really hot. He had bigger and better coming his way, and very soon.

Danny Street walked back into Kokomo's Café, where a new set of customers were waiting to congratulate him for his coming success.

Custom Machine

Mac was standing on the front deck, sneaking in a cigarette and watching the tourists and locals mixing on the boardwalk to the east, a couple of blocks away. It had been a good day. Not only because he'd sold quite a few sandwiches and cups of coffee, but because the time had flown by and he only had a few hours left. He couldn't wait for the doors to be locked so he could really relax, go see this house with Ginny, and then crack open a cold one and sit in his favorite chair and smoke a few cigarettes before bed. He loved the simple life Kokomo's Café afforded him and his family. He wouldn't trade this in for the world.

He heard the roar of a motorcycle somewhere, coming over the bridge on Moody Avenue, and closed his eyes, remembering his younger days, tooling around on a bike with his hair flipping in the breeze. He put his hand on his head, rubbing his prominent bald spot. The long hair was long gone, and the years of drinking beer had brought him a beer gut.

It was a few bikes, and they were getting closer. Mac walked down the steps to the street and looked north, just as the first Harley pulled onto South Central from Moody, riding past the park. It was followed by two more bikes.

They drove up, slowly, and parked in front of Kokomo's Café, Mac stepping back up the steps to get out of the way. *Sweet rides*, he thought, knowing he was sounding like an old man. But he didn't care. He was about to ask them about the bikes, all custom jobs, when he saw the tell-tale rocker patches on their jackets: Black Death MC's. These dudes were bad asses, and usually stayed closer to Daytona Beach. He didn't like them up in his neck of the woods, especially this late in the day.

As they took their time dismounting and talking, Mac casually hopped up the steps and went inside. "I think trouble just pulled up," he said to his wife. "Put the phone nearby and get ready to call 9-1-1 if there's a problem."

"What's going on?"

Mac was glad they were currently slow, with no one hanging out in the main room or at the counter, besides the quiet guy in the corner. He glanced into the side room and saw Danny Street. "Hey, you might want to skirt out the back door. I think we're going to have a problem with some bikers."

"No way." Danny looked at his watch. "The manager should be here in the next hour. I'm going to relax back here." He had his feet up on the table and his chair leaning against a wall.

Stupid kid. "Suit yourself, but if we start yelling, you need to split." Mac went to go into the kitchen. "And get your feet off my table."

* * * * *

Bones went to the counter and smiled at the woman. She was a couple years older than him but looked damn good for her age, and had a twinkle in her eye. She guessed the dude in the kitchen, watching him slyly and holding the serrated knife, was her old man. "Can I get three coffees?"

"Sure, coming right up."

"Grab me a chocolate chip muffin, too," Tank said. He was seated at the table across from the counter. "Make it two."

Coop stood and went to the pastry display. "What the heck is that?"

The woman smiled. "They are chocolate covered bacon strips."

"You kidding me?"

"No. Would you like one?"

Bones laughed. "Heck, I'll take all six of them. That sounds amazing."

"You're going to share them," Coop said.

"It depends on what they taste like." Bones watched the woman, as she poured the coffees. If they weren't here for important business, he'd flirt with her a bit and see if she was interested in slipping away from her husband for a few hours of fun. Every chick liked a biker and a ride up and down the coast.

He'd met quite a few women, standing behind a counter, day in and day out, who longed to run away from their boring lives and see the open highway. They'd party, drink and do crazy shit. At some point, they'd wake up and see themselves in the mirror and freak out. They always did. That's when the party would be over, and Bones would drop them back outside their front door and never see them again. And, he was fine with it.

"Ginny, did this order want red onions and tomato?" her husband said, still holding the knife, as he called out.

"Yes, dear." Ginny turned back to Bones. "Anything else, sir?"

"I think we're good for now. Can we sit out back?"

"Of course." She put the muffins and chocolate covered bacon on the counter with the coffees and rang him up. "It's nice out back this time of day."

Bones handed her two twenties and told her to keep the change.

"Are you sure?" When he nodded, she thanked him.

"I'm not carrying all this by myself. Get up and help," Bones said. "Or it's mine. I paid for it."

* * * * *

"Will you stop?" Ginny said to Mac, who was stealing peeks out the kitchen window, overlooking the back deck.

Mac waved her off. "I don't trust them."

"They were just a group of guys who came in for coffee and chocolate covered bacon. You're being paranoid. They were actually very nice. Suddenly, you don't like bikers?"

"Don't you watch the news? These guys are bad people. They're gun smugglers, drug dealers and killers. What if they decide they want the cash register?"

"I pop it open, smile and give them the cash. What else can you do? Some little old lady might walk in here and rip us off. Heck, we lost another roll of toilet paper today. I think it's the young girl who sits out front and reads. This is the second day in a row."

"I'm not talking about toilet paper, or those two weird girls who spread salt all around the table and then stole the salt shaker. Remember that weird shit?"

Ginny laughed. "Some people are crazy."

Mac looked back out. "They're just sitting there."

"Eating and drinking? What bastards."

Mac grinned. "You know what I mean. They're up to no good."

The back door opened and Mac shot across the small kitchen, grabbing the knife.

Ginny laughed and went back, out just as the first biker came in.

"Can I get a refill on the coffee? And, I gotta tell you, the bacon is amazing. Is there anymore hidden back there?"

"Sorry. As quick as we make it, it's gone. My husband eats half of it, too. He loves it." Ginny filled his coffee cup. "I'll make some more for next weekend."

"I'll be back. Make a lot of it, too. I could live on that for a week."

"Are you nuts?" Mac asked, when he went back out the door. "Don't tell him you're making more for next weekend."

"I never thought of that," Ginny said and mock-gasped. "They might come back and buy them. We can't have customers coming back again and again."

Mac shook his head. "You know what I mean."

"Not really. I think if they were going to kill us, they would have done it by now. Instead, they want more coffee. They even tipped us pretty big."

"So did the biker guy from this afternoon."

"Maybe they were in cahoots. He was advanced scouting you. They probably want to kidnap you and see if I'll pay a ransom," Ginny said.

"Man, I'd be screwed, huh?"

"Pretty much. Now stop waving the stupid knife at me and relax. We still have customers."

* * * * *

"Mind if I put this flyer up in the window?" the redhead asked with a smile.

Ginny took it from her and read it. "We have our own roller derby team in Palm Coast?"

"Yes. We've been here almost four years, but only started bouting in the last year." She extended her hand. "I'm Amber, but they call me Ginger N Juicy. We're trying to get people excited about us. Right now, we play in Ormond Beach for home games but we're trying to figure out a place closer to home so the local Palm Coast and Flagler Beach fans don't have to travel so far."

"Good luck. I'll hang it up. My husband's mom was a roller derby girl, right Mac?"

He was busy staring out the side window at the bikers. Ginny sighed. "His mom loved it. I remember seeing all her pictures from back in the day. I've never been, but it looks neat. I loved roller-skating. My daughter, Marie, trail skates in Palm Coast."

"I might know her. I'm out there every weekend, when we don't have a bout. Is she a perky blonde?"

"That's my Marie."

"I think one of the girls talked to her about it, but she's in college right now?"

"She's between semesters, but she goes to school full-time and works here with us. Marie is a really good skater, but she's probably too small for your team."

Amber stood back and smiled, pointing at her full figure. "Luckily, all the teams we bout against aren't built like me. We have a few girls smaller than Marie but they are really fast. It doesn't matter what your size is as long as you keep from getting hit. And, luckily, she'd have me on her side, because I can put a check on the opposition."

"Mac, are you listening?" Ginny asked. She laughed when he ran away from the window again, as the back door opened.

The biker came back in with two empty coffee cups. "Refills, please." He grinned at Amber. "Hello there, Red."

"Hi." Amber turned away, her face matching her hair.

"I'm Bones." He handed Ginny the two cups.

"I'm Ginger N Juicy."

"That's an odd name."

"You mean like Bones?"

He nodded. "Would you believe my parents named me that?"

"Not for a second. I'm, actually, Amber, but my roller derby name is Ginger N Juicy."

Bones pointed at the flyer. "I figured as much. Roller derby is hot." He winked. "And roller derby women."

She blushed again.

"Are you local? Maybe we could go for a ride this afternoon or Sunday," he said.

Ginny put the two filled cups of coffee on the counter and went into the kitchen.

"It depends. What's your real name?"

Bones smiled. "There's only two ways for you to find that out."

"I'm waiting."

Bones put up a finger. "If you're a cop." He held up two fingers. "Or, I tell you the morning after. If you aren't a cop..."

"It was nice meeting you, Bones. Good luck with both of those." Amber turned to the owners in the kitchen. "Thank you." She went out the front door without looking back at Bones.

*   *   *   *   *

"When you're done playing detective, I have some orders for you. Are you too busy to work now? Should I call for backup?" Ginny asked.

Mac frowned at her and took the slips from her hand. "They're waiting for someone."

"I didn't know you went out and had a conversation with them."

He pointed at the kitchen window, where he'd spent the last twenty minutes. "The one guy is leaning on the rail and keeps looking up and down the side street. The other one is looking the other way, while the big one is sitting and keeps looking at his watch."

"So, three guys enjoying a lazy Friday afternoon with coffee and muffins are looking around? I'll call the F.B.I."

Mac wagged a finger. "Mark my words: they are up to no good. This will be some kind of drug deal or something. The cops are probably watching them, and now they're watching Kokomo's. We're in the middle of this."

"They'll say you're the mastermind, honey." Ginny went to her husband and hugged him. "You won't do well in prison. You're too pretty."

"Sometimes, you drive me crazy," he said and squeezed his wife. "But, I'm sure something is up."

"You didn't say a word this morning when the other biker guy beat the crap out of the guy in the alley."

"Yeah, but he seemed nice enough."

Ginny laughed. "He was a monster."

"He had his reasons for beating those guys up, and he, technically, did it on the sidewalk. I'm not getting involved in a personal argument, but these three are using my back deck as a drug ring front."

"I love how dramatic you get."

"Watch and wait."

"In the meantime, Kojak, I need these orders done."

*　　*　　*　　*　　*

"I knew it," Mac hissed as he ran out of the kitchen. His gut instincts were hardly ever wrong, and now he had the proof. "Another guy just showed up."

"Isn't four guys on the back deck illegal? I'll alert the media," Ginny said.

"You can joke it up all you want, but I'm calling the police." Mac grabbed for the phone.

"What are you doing?"

"Come here, and bring the phone with you." Mac ran to the back window and peeked out. "See?"

"What am I looking... oh." Ginny moved back from the window.

Mac put his hand out for the phone. "I told you."

The newest member of the group was standing near the rail holding a rifle case, a long black leather one. All four men were huddled around it and smiling, talking excitedly.

Ginny was peeking out the window. "I can't see inside it from this angle."

"Get away from there before they see you. If they know you know what they are doing, they'll snuff us out." Mac dialed 9-1-1.

"Should we get everyone out of the building?" Ginny asked.

Mac shook his head. "If they see everyone leaving, they'll know something is up. Go see if you can casually get everyone to leave and get to safety. I don't want to put anyone in danger, but I don't want them trapped inside when these maniacs start shooting."

"They won't do that... will they?"

"I need you guy's down here now. Kokomo's Café on South Central. I have four Black Death Motorcycle gang members making a gun deal on my back deck, and I have a crowd of customers." Mac waved for Ginny to go. "Get to safety."

66

Ginny went in, around and in front of the counter, and looked about to talk to a couple seated there, when she turned back to Mac and began pointing, excitedly, at the back door. "They're leaving!"

"The gang is on the move," Mac said to the police dispatcher. He skirted to the counter, keeping low. "There are four of them, and I have no idea how many rifles are in the case."

Ginny put her face to the back door and looked through the glass. "They went between us and Bahama Mama's. I hope they leave."

Mac was giving a play by play, on the phone, as he ran to the front door, startling a few customers. The guy in the corner, briefly, looked up from his laptop, before burying his face back down into whatever it was he was working on.

The three original bikers went to their Harleys, the one who called himself Bones holding the gun case. Mac watched the other guy walk down the sidewalk and out of sight. At least, they were leaving. Mac didn't want to think about these madmen inside his business with firearms and innocent people.

Mac hung up the phone when the dispatcher told him units were en route. He just hoped they got here in time, before someone crossed their path.

"What did they say?" Ginny asked, gripping his hand and pushing up against his back.

"They're on the way. I can't believe this."

The motorcycles were started and the three bikers pulled away, heading south with a roar.

Mac went out onto the sidewalk and watched as they turned east on South Fourth Street, heading to A1A. As the first Sheriffs car pulled up, lights flashing, Mac pointed east and south. The car was joined by another and they sped off.

"Now we wait, and hope they catch them," Mac said to Ginny and went back inside.

* * * * *

Officer Travis Armstrong walked into Kokomo's Café and went right to the counter, where Ginny and Mac were standing. He looked completely serious, which didn't bode well. Travis was a local, who'd gone to Flagler Palm Coast High School with their son Brandon, and had been over their house dozens of times.

"You're not smiling," Ginny said.

Travis looked around the room, eyes locked on the guy in the corner for a moment. "Can we talk in the side room?"

"Sure," Mac said.

The three went into the side room, but Danny Street was alone in the room, his feet up on the table and his eyes closed.

"Get your feet off my table," Mac shouted, a bit louder than he intended, but he was excited and scared, right now. He wanted to know what happened.

Travis led the couple into the kitchen.

"Shit, Travis, what happened?" Mac finally asked, as the officer kept staring at them.

"I'm not sure how to tell you this. Can I get a cup of coffee?"

"Huh? Sure," Mac said.

After a moment, Travis put his hands up. "Can I get it now, sir?"

Mac shook his head and crossed his arms. "Spill the beans, kid. Then you'll get all the coffee you want."

"We pulled the gang over, off of A1A, onto 18th Street. The one with the rifle case looked like he wanted to run. I had my hand on my holster..."

When Travis closed his eyes, Mac leaned against the wall.

"And?" Ginny asked, breaking the silence.

Travis opened his eyes. "He popped the rifle case open and pulled out a piece, the size of which I've never seen before."

"Oh, God," Mac said. This was worse than he thought.

"And then he broke, and he ended up running the pool table," their son Brandon said from the other side of the counter.

Mac was confused. What the hell was he talking about? When Travis and Brandon started laughing, he knew this wasn't going to be good. "Tell me," he said but he didn't want to know.

"I'm really, really sorry. Brandon made me do it. They had a customized pool cue case, made to look like a rifle case. They were actually pretty cool about it and we laughed. It was a false alarm, but they realized how it looked with him driving down the road with it. They had no idea you'd called, thinking we saw them."

"So you called this idiot?" Mac asked, pointing at his son, who was dressed in his Flagler Fish Company shirt. "He left work for this?"

"Of course, I did. Why would I miss this fun?"

Ginny pointed at Mac. "First, he's your kid. Same stupid sense of humor. Second, I told you they weren't doing anything wrong."

Mac threw his hands up. "I can't win."

"Can I get a cup of coffee now?" Travis asked.

Mac smiled. "Get out."

Love Is a Woman

Marco Petrucci couldn't stop smiling.

"You want me to leave room for cream and sugar?" Ginny asked.

Chazz looked at Marco, who was staring out the window and smiling. "Dude, you want her to leave room?"

Marco had just met the girl of his dreams, and she was either playing hard to get or she was the biggest bitch he'd ever met. Either way, it was love at first sight. He stared outside and imagined her walking up with that gorgeous smile, watching him watch her.

Chazz punched him in the arm, pulling Marco back to reality.

"Really? Did you just hit me?"

"Wake up. You've been all stupid since lunch." Chazz pulled his hand back to throw another punch but Marco stood up and got into a boxing stance.

"Boys..." Ginny said. "Not in here."

The two men, in their mid-twenties, laughed and went to the counter.

They grabbed the two coffees off the counter and Marco handed Ginny a twenty. "Keep the change."

Ginny looked at him confused. "It's four dollars and change."

Marco waved her off and sat back down, face pressed to the window.

"What are you looking at?" Chazz asked.

"I'm wondering where she is." Marco thought about seeing her, just an hour ago, at the Golden Lion.

* * * * *

"I'm Woody. What can I get you tourists?" the bartender asked, with a smile and a laugh, adjusting his Fun Coast Bartending cap.

"Tourists? We're locals," Chazz said with a laugh.

"Your pale skin, Jersey accents and the fact you're checking out every woman in the place like you've never seen a sun-kissed hot chick tells me differently. What are you drinking?"

"What do you suggest?" Marco asked. They'd only been in Florida a few hours but already he loved it. Flagler Beach was off the main trail, set between the spring break crowd of Daytona Beach and the old world charm of Saint Augustine, and felt like the perfect hideaway for their trip.

"Two Miami Sunsets coming up," Woody said with a grin. He tossed a menu on the counter of the tiki bar. "If you're hungry, I can take your order, too. A couple of these and you'll need something to eat."

"We're from Jersey. We know how to handle a drink, buddy." Chazz turned to Marco. "This guy thinks he's funny. We might need to take him behind the dumpster and mess him up."

"Relax. We're on vacation. Just enjoy the scenery. Try not to be your loud and obnoxious self for once."

"What are you trying to say?"

"I'm trying to say the reason we're even here is because of you."

Chazz scrunched his face, his thick eyebrows meeting, and got close to Marco. "Bullshit. How the fuck was I to know the Baker kid was armed to the teeth? He drew and I took him down."

"There was no reason, and he didn't pull his gun. He put his hand on his jacket to remind you he had it when you started getting stupid."

"I was getting annoyed they were taking so long to make the handoff."

Marco shook his head. "We shouldn't have even been there. I'm a computer guy, and you're... related to the boss."

Chazz laughed. "I thought we did good for our first run. The next will go smoother."

"Again: I'm a computer guy. I hack into accounts and steal from faceless people. I can make you a birth certificate or license. I can steal from Peter and give to Pauly but the next time something last minute comes up I want you to keep me out of it. I'm serious. I'm not that guy. I want to fly under the radar. You brought so much bad heat to us it's unreal. You think your uncle told us to take a vacation because we did well? He got us out of town and told me to take you and get as far away from Newark as possible."

Woody placed two coasters and drinks on the bar. "I'll set you two locals up with a tab?"

Marco nodded. He took a sip. "This shit is good. Bourbon and Triple Sec with orange juice, and a Grenadine sinker. Up north, we use tequila instead of Triple Sec, but this is smooth."

Chazz ignored the straw and slammed his in three mighty gulps, wiping his mouth with his sleeve. "It's alright."

The bartender stared at Chazz with a big grin on his face.

"What's so fucking funny, Drink Boy?"

"Chazz, lighten the fuck up. Don't make a scene," Marco said. He didn't want to start trouble. He wanted to blend in, keep a low profile, and then figure out what his move was going to be when they returned to Newark. The last thing he wanted was for his lifelong buddy to, once again, get them in trouble.

"How was the drink, tough guy?" Woody asked.

"How about I come over the counter and fuck you up?" Chazz said, loudly.

Marco grabbed his arm. "I'm not kidding, man. Drop this shit before we get tossed out of here. I'm warning you. I'm sure your dad will not be happy you got us heat, in two different states, in the same week. Do you understand me?"

Chazz was fuming but looked at Marco. "Let me smoke this bitch and we can go somewhere else."

"No." Marco tossed a twenty on the bar. "I think we're done."

"You haven't finished your drink," Woody said with a smile.

Marco wasn't going to create a scene but this guy was being a dick. "Look, buddy, I don't know what your fucking game is, but I'm not getting baited." Marco looked around. "Let me guess: you have a couple of Neanderthal bouncers in this place, or the two biker-wannabe douche bags on the other side of the bar are going to jump in for you? I'm not here to play local bullshit tough guy games, got it? I'll walk away and you can keep smiling. Or I let my boy here off his leash and he breaks your arm - and he *will* break your fucking arm - before anyone can bounce. Then we burn this bitch to the ground."

Woody's eyes were getting wider and wider as Marco was talking. He put his hands up, waving them. "Holy crap, no way. I meant no offense, I swear. I was just playing around with you guys since you're from up North. I'm a Chicago guy. I thought you'd see I was joking." Woody offered a hand to Marco. "Seriously, my bad. This round is on me."

Marco smiled. He'd be tough when he needed to be. He took Woody's hand and squeezed, shaking it and holding on a couple of extra seconds. *I'm in control, not you.* "No harm, no foul, right? I'll get another one of these. Pretty good shit."

Chazz went to open his mouth and Marco punched his arm.

"Really? Did you hit me?"

"Very much so. I need you to shut up and sit back and stare at the local chicks."

"I'd rather punch this loser out," Chazz said.

"And miss out on getting some easy Florida chicks? There is something wrong with you, bro. I'm here to get laid. If you want to act all manly and fight another dude, maybe roll around in the sand with him, knock yourself out. I'm going to drink another couple of these drinks and get a nice buzz and then wander around and flash my baby blue eyes and my winning smile. I'd rather crawl out of some chick's bed than share a hotel room with you, anyway. Of course, while you're slapping your bartender boyfriend around, I can use both beds in the hotel to nail some Florida va-jay-jay."

"Point taken."

"You think he has nice lips? Is that why you want to fight him? Big arms? Sexy shoulders?"

"Fuck off, dude." Chazz smiled at Woody when he put two more drinks on the bar but checked himself when Marco started laughing. "I swear you are the only person who can get away with saying shit like that to me. My own mother would get a black eye for half the shit you say to me."

"Maybe you're in love with me, too."

"I swear, as God is my witness…"

Marco put his hands up with a grin. "Let's just chill. This is fucking paradise. Get in a better mood."

* * * * *

Chazz ordered another drink, his fourth, and he looked like wasn't feeling a thing. The bartender hadn't been kidding: these drinks were killer. Marco sipped his second and was happy just watching the crowd.

The Golden Lion was packed, and there were many women in skimpy bikinis and revealing outfits walking around, smiling and making sure every male head was turned in their direction.

"This is the life. I might even be sad getting back on the plane Sunday night," Chazz slurred.

"Are you drunk?"

"Nope." Chazz grinned. "Yep."

"Slow down. It's too early. Are you hungry?"

"I could eat. Maybe we'll order some appetizers and some burgers. I could use some onion rings."

Marco stood up and pointed at Woody. "Let your boyfriend know we're ready to order. Get me a cheeseburger and fries. Maybe some mozzarella sticks, and an iced tea."

"Where you going?"

"Can I take a piss by myself?"

"I guess."

The walk to the bathroom took a few minutes since the bottom outside was swamped with people. *This is a great little place,* Marco thought. He was going to miss it. They might just end up hanging here the next two days, since it seemed to be the center of the universe for hot chicks.

Marco saw her, sitting at one of the picnic tables close to the building, with another girl. Blonde hair, huge smile, sparkling eyes.

"Wow," he actually whispered. He stopped and watched her as she laughed at her friend's joke. She was in her mid-twenties, dressed in a white and blue sundress and wearing flip flops. Marco knew she wasn't like the rest of the women around here. She was full-figured and comfortable in her own skin. She was... damn, she was just smoking hot.

She glanced in his direction and their eyes met.

Marco smiled. Beautiful. She was tan and her flowing blonde hair came down her shoulders, just the hint of her neck showing. He had the urge to run and kiss her neck and red lips. He felt like a kid again.

"Can I help you?" she asked him.

Marco smiled but she didn't return it.

"Hello? Is there a problem?"

74

"I'm just… you are very pretty," he managed, waiting for her eyes to light up at the compliment.

"I'll let my parents know they did well." She turned to her friend. "Seriously? Are all Yankees like this?"

Her friend was smiling and shook her head. "Not all of them. But, definitely, this one, Chelle."

"Chelle? That's a pretty name."

"My name is Michelle. My friends call me Chelle."

"I'm Marco. Nice to meet you, Chelle."

"You can't call me Chelle, and you need to find another word besides pretty, although, it does fit when talking about me."

Marco felt his face turning red and, quickly, exited to the bathroom, where he splashed water on his face. He'd just been dissed hard, and he didn't like it. *This chick has no idea who I am*, he thought. *Back home I can get every woman I look at and she is making fun of me? How dare she.* Marco was going to compose himself and then go out there and walk right past her like she didn't exist. He wouldn't look in her direction, and even if she smiled at him or waved him over, he'd ignore her.

Marco marched past their table, but the two women were laughing and sharing a joke. *Probably talking about me*, he thought. *Let them. I'll stick in her head and she'll be looking at me.*

Chazz had a full drink in front of him and was talking to a redhead with overlarge, fake boobs and a glazed look in her eyes. Her friend, a brunette, looked like she'd gone to the same plastic surgeon and asked for a matching pair. "Hey, where ya been? Marco, I want you to meet our new friends. This is…"

"I'm Scarlet and this is my friend, Raven," the redhead said.

Marco wanted to ask what strip club they danced at and if they gave each other the stupid stripper names, but decided against it. Instead, he said hi and looked away when the brunette licked her lips at him and awkwardly tried to grab at his arm, before gravity and her drunken state made her miss.

Chazz slurped his drink and grinned. "The girls live close by. I'm thinking we take this party to their place, and have some real fun."

Marco took two steps to his left, away from the girls, so he could see Michelle. *I need to work on getting to call her Chelle*, he thought. *I need to get to know her.* Marco knew, as cliché as it sounded, this was love at first sight. This was the reason he was here. He didn't know if he believed in fate and karma and all that, but he, instinctively, knew this was happening for a reason. What was the chance he'd need a break from his life, come down to a random town he knew nothing about in order to hide and regroup, and then find a woman so beautiful it made him stop in his tracks? Marco had been with many, many women in his life, but none of them intrigued him like this one.

She wasn't in the chair.

He panicked, moving toward the table, ignoring Chazz as he yelled for him. Where was she? He spotted her blonde hair, heading to the exit, and ran to intercept her. Marco had no idea what he was going to say when he stopped her.

* * * * *

"You can't be serious," Chazz said, as he downed his coffee. "The big blonde chick? I saw her. She's nothing special. Damn, we could have been banging the two hot chicks right now, but you blew it. I'm supposed to be the rude one, not you."

"I'm not interested in another one night stand and another meaningless conquest."

"Since when?"

"Since I saw Michelle."

Chazz laughed, almost spitting out the last of his coffee. "Man, I don't get you. There are a hundred chicks hotter than her on this beach. You can throw a stick and hit two amazing blondes. And since when do you like blondes? I thought redheads were your thing, and skinnier chicks, at that."

"I'm so bored with women, and… this one is different. I can't explain it."

"You'll never be able to. I won't ever get it. I think you're wasting your time. Did you get her number? Did you get anything concrete from her? Maybe a smile?"

"She did smile," Marco said, quickly, but she really didn't smile at *him* per se. Still, she did smile. And it was a great smile.

"Regardless, you need to lighten up and enjoy the chicks throwing themselves at us. The local chicks are hot, and readily available."

"I'm not interested," Marco said.

"Are you telling me you're going to waste the next two days, moping around and pining for a chick that doesn't even care about you? She's probably home right now with her boyfriend, or you're just a fading idiot she'll forget about within the hour. Dude, you need to have some fun while we're here. You're going to get on the plane, after a wasted weekend, and talk about all the chicks we could have banged."

Marco stared out the window. A couple was walking in the park, and he saw a young man across the street head into Nerdz Comics And More. He was followed by a girl, probably his girlfriend, and they were both smiling.

"You haven't touched your coffee. I'm going to switch back to beer. They have the Batch 19 stuff, ever had it? Pre-Prohibition recipe. It's really good. Want one, instead? I don't know why we stopped drinking." Chazz stood up. "Oh, wait... because you are suddenly afraid of getting laid and nailing random babes."

"I'm not leaving," Marco said, simply.

"I'll get the beer, God forbid you get off your ass."

Marco turned to Chazz and smiled. "No, I mean I'm not going back to New Jersey."

"Bullshit."

"I'm going to stay and settle here. I can't keep doing what I'm doing."

"You can't do that. Chenzo will come down here and drag you back, by your pretty hair. We don't work for Walmart; we work for the mob. You're joking."

"Chenzo has no idea where we are."

"Sure he does."

"Did you tell him?"

Chazz shook his head. "No, but he knew we were coming down here."

"No, he thinks we're in San Diego, right now. I traded in our tickets in Newark and we flew here. I don't ever tell you shit, so you can't be questioned. I need you to keep your mouth shut."

"I'm going back to get my ass kicked, you know. I'm not that stupid. I realize I fucked up again, and there will be hell to pay when I get back. I was hoping you could go to bat for me, yet again, and save my ass. Without you getting my back, I'm screwed."

"Then stay."

"And do what?"

Marco grinned. "Drink beer, bang local chicks, make up a new identity. Shit, we do that for a living."

"If you go entrepreneur down here, they'll bury us. Literally."

"We don't need to. How much cash you have on you?"

"I dunno, two grand? Not much."

"I have about five. I say we clean out the bank accounts and live with cash. I have another seventy-five in a stash account, and thirty-five in my other spot. I know, damn well, you have some saved for a rainy day."

"Eighty."

"You know how long we can live off the money we have? And we can live well here, and no one will ever know."

"I don't know about this."

Marco leaned forward. "If you get off a plane in Newark, Chenzo is going to break your legs. Or worse. This is a sign from God we need to cut the ties. I'm not talking about cutting into their work or even getting back into the business. We have enough of a nest egg to live comfortably for a long time."

"We don't have a car, and no place to stay."

"Cash is king. We buy a non-descript car and rent a bungalow in town and pay six months in advance and a big deposit."

"Are you really thinking of doing this?"

"I'm beyond thinking about it. I'm going to do it."

"I'm going home."

Marco shook his head. "They'll hurt you."

"Maybe I deserve it. I keep fucking up. They are also family. That has to count for something. Just come back, face the heat with me, and then you can leave on your terms."

"They'll never let me walk away." Marco smiled. "This isn't Walmart. You don't put in your two week notice. They'll find another computer guy and won't miss a beat. I'm going to mail them the codes for everything and won't touch a dime in the accounts. They'll have no reason to follow me."

"And when they ask me?"

"You tell them the truth: I ducked out in San Diego, when I met a skinny redhead stripper, and headed to Vegas. I'll be back once I sober up."

"That will only buy you a few weeks, on the outside."

"It will give me plenty of time."

"For what?"

Marco looked out the window again. "To find Chelle."

Here Comes the Night

Wayne Tursha was a big man. He parked his Jaguar in front of Kokomo's Café and pulled himself from the car, which he, literally, filled. Even though it was getting late, he needed to get out of the stifling heat of Florida. This trip was already taking too long.

He checked his Rolex. He had six hours before his plane, in Jacksonville, took off, and there was no way he was missing it.

"This snot-nosed punk better be worth my time," he said, between gasps. When he stumbled up the steps, his weight threatening to crush the wood beneath him, his face was a mask of sweat.

The customers openly stared when he entered, a giant sweat-ball with crazy purple hair, big, thick, white sunglasses and a white suit. Wayne smiled, loving the dramatic entrance he always made.

Twenty-four hours ago he was in a meeting with Rob Thomas of Matchbox 20 fame, going over a tour idea his company was working on. Today, he hoped he'd strike gold again, this time getting in on the ground floor with this kid. He needed to sign him, today, before Classic Management could sink their teeth into him. This kid came with a shitload of solid songs he owned (although Wayne could already see a dozen loopholes to pull them from Danny Street), and he had a look the pop and country girls would love.

Everyone went back to their own business, as Wayne trudged to the counter. "I'm here to meet a Danny Street," he said and laughed to himself at the stupid rhyme. He filed the sentence in his mind, thinking he could use it, in the future, on posters, when they did those boring meet and greet in-store appearances.

The man behind the counter smiled. "He's in the side room. He's been expecting you. Would you like something to drink?"

Wayne glanced up at the high shelf, holding the beers they carried. "What's cold right now?"

"I have all of them on ice."

He tapped a meaty finger on his goatee, which was currently red with light purple streaks throughout. "How about we start with Angry Orchard and Batch 19?"

"Both?"

"Yes, sir. Two of each." He looked over the pastry display case. "And the carrot cake looks awesome. Give me what's left of the one in the back."

Mac laughed. "That's half the cake."

"I'll take it."

*　*　*　*　*

Danny kept the smile plastered on his face, as he watched the huge man eating the carrot cake, between sips of beer. So far, they'd introduced themselves but Mr. Tursha had told him to relax before they got into the meeting because he needed to eat and drink really quickly. He wasn't kidding, shoveling the cake into his mouth with the tiny fork in his big hand.

Wayne finished his fourth beer and called for Mac. "Can I get another two rounds, dear?" Wayne turned to Danny. "You need a refill?"

"Sure."

"Give the kid whatever he wants," Wayne said and went back to the last of the cake.

Kid? Danny didn't like being called a kid, especially by this guy. By anyone. He was an adult and demanded respect, but he wasn't about to do anything to jeopardize the million dollar deal that was coming. Danny smiled and leaned back in the chair, trying to appear casual. This fat dude needed to think Danny was in command and comfortable with this initial meeting.

Mac put the four new beers on the table and took the empties, as well as the empty plate and fork.

Wayne Tursha grinned and slapped his palms together. "Let's get down to the nitty gritty, shall we?"

"I'm looking forward to this meeting."

"Meeting? Ha, I don't have time for meetings. I'm a busy man. I'm flying back to New York to put together the next Taylor Swift production team. Wayne Tursha doesn't fly a thousand miles to feel someone out. I've done my research, and I know you have, too. You talked to people in the business, you went online and did your own looking around, and you know damn well Tursha Management is the right fit for Danny Street and his music." He pulled out a folded set of papers, from his inside jacket pocket, and a gold pen and placed them on the table between Danny and his beers. "Take a look and let me know what you think. The percents are generous for a first-time talent, and you'll find the budgets for everything also in line with you being an unknown."

Danny picked up the papers and scanned the top sheet, but most of what was written was in legal mumbo jumbo. He tried to look like he was studying it, but he had no idea what he was reading. "What is the bottom line for this?" he, finally, asked and put the papers down in front of him.

Wayne smiled, a beer in hand. "The bottom line, kid? I'm going to make you a fucking star, a household name. I'll have every teenage girl and their MILF moms creaming in their thongs over you. I'll have you on the country music charts within the year, and we'll be seeing your pretty mug on the cover of every major magazine."

This is really happening, Danny thought. *All this hard work, all the shitty coffee shops, bowling alleys, grand opening events, outdoor parks with bad sound, and clubs in Orlando and Jacksonville, all done for this moment.*

Wayne pushed the paper closer to him and handed him the pen. "Just sign the last page and initial everywhere I highlighted. I'll have a limo pick you up on Monday morning and you can fly up to New York. Ever met Usher?"

"No."

Wayne finished his beer, slamming it back onto the table. "He found that little kid online and made him into a star. I can do you bigger and better. Your songs are tighter and don't need as much work to make them great. I'm pulling in a couple of hotshots from Nahsville."

"I just got back from there," Danny said.

Wayne looked annoyed and pursed his lips before speaking. "Forget the shit you did in Nashville. Those guys will rip you off. I heard one of the songs, and they sound like shit. They don't get you and your music. I do, and my staff will work with you to develop not only the right sound, but the right look. It's all about branding.

You need to be created over again, in the proper image. We'll accentuate your boyish good looks. How old are you?"

Before Danny could answer, Wayne put up a finger. "You are twenty-one. Just turned the legal age, when we make the announcements. That will drive the girls and their mom's crazy. We need to get you a proper haircut, though. And some nice clothes. We'll fly you to Los Angeles and get a complete makeover. I know someone who will go nuts over your raw looks."

"I can get other songs, too. I know a guy who writes in the same style as I do," Danny said. If he could get Wade to relax and see the big picture, he could get a few more songs out of him. The more the merrier.

"Nah, we're going to trunk the tunes you have for now. I have a team already putting a catalogue together for you, with your singing voice and style in mind. We can churn out an album's worth of great songs in a weekend. I'm not worried about the music. I'm worried about the Package. We need to get you set up and ready to go."

"I'm ready."

Wayne looked down at the contract. "Then start signing and we can begin."

"I need to read it first, though, right?"

"Sure, take your time." Wayne looked at his Rolex. "I have to fly out to Iowa today and sit down with another country singer. He's about your age… your basic look, but he's already signed. I just need to pick up the contract and he's coming back with me, to New York, to meet with Usher and Kenny Chesney. Ken wants to do a duet with the kid, and I think it would be a huge hit."

"I love Kenny Chesney; he is such an inspiration to my writing," Danny lied.

Wayne tapped his lip and stared at Danny. "I'd rather put you in the studio with Ken, but…"

Danny grabbed the contract and leafed through it quickly, scanning random spots. He got to the end and signed it.

"There are a bunch of other clauses you need to initial," Wayne said and pointed them out, page by page. When Danny was done, Wayne snatched it off the table, went through it again, and tucked it back in his jacket pocket.

"It was great doing business with you. I will have someone e-mail you with the details for Monday. Make sure you pack for cooler weather." Wayne stood up and smiled. "I'll see you in New York, and we'll unleash Danny Street, on the world."

Danny laughed. "This is so cool."

"Yes, it is." Wayne turned to leave.

"Um, Mister Tursha… the beer and food needs to be paid for."

Wayne kept walking. "Save the receipt and we'll reimburse you when you get to New York. Make sure you save everything, or you won't get paid."

*   *   *   *   *

Mac watched out the big window at the activity going on at Veteran's Park. The First Friday event would be in full swing soon enough, but he wouldn't be going over to enjoy it. He had a date with Ginny and a house when he closed up. She'd gone ahead of him, excited and looking forward to seeing the potential new place.

"Time to wrap up another day," Mac called out to the quiet guy in the corner. "There's always Monday."

As the man packed up his laptop and papers and rolled all his various wires up and tucked them into his computer bag, Mac pulled out the broom and swept in front of the counter.

When he was done, he did a quick peek into the back room, making sure no one else was around. The bathroom was empty, and he wiped it down and dumped the small garbage can into the larger one behind the counter. He shut down the coffee and espresso machines, made sure the kitchen was clean and all the garbage was accounted for, before tying up the bag and placing it next to the back door. The television went off, the radio following.

Mac had his routine for closing down to a science, and he could get everything done and in order within fifteen minutes. He worked quicker when he closed by himself, which wasn't usual. Ginny or Marie just got in his way, not understanding the method to his madness. Once the quiet guy left, he'd lock the door behind him, click the back door, and do a sweep of the rest of Kokomo's Café, before a last check of the kitchen and behind the counter.

He kept stealing glances out the front window, because it was always about this time of day when someone walked up and wanted to hang out and sip coffee so he couldn't go home. It never failed.

So far, so good. The deck was empty, and he slipped out and grabbed all the salt and pepper shakers, checking for trash as he went. It was still beautiful outside, a nice ocean breeze stirring the OPEN flags as he furled them.

"I'll see you Monday."

"Yeah, have a good weekend." Mac said. "What are you writing, anyway? Everyone is so interested in the secretive guy sitting in the corner."

He smiled, stroking his graying bushy goatee. "I'm writing about nothing."

"Like *Seinfeld*?"

The man chuckled. "Yeah, something like that. Good luck with the house. Today was very busy, which worked out nicely for me."

Author Notes

The initial idea for the Flagler Beach Fiction Series was conceived when a small-press publisher approached me through a third party and asked if I had any ideas for a Contemporary Fiction book.

"Of course!" I said, having no idea what Contemporary Fiction actually encompassed. I had to Google it between e-mails. "Yeah, easy enough."

I'm a horror writer. Sure, I've written a few non-fiction books and some thrillers, but in my stories people tend to die. Zombies, guns, demons... you get the idea.

I liked the challenge of writing stories based on characters. Where the action (while still there at times) was backseat to the people themselves.

Flagler Beach is a quirky little Florida town, filled with unique individuals and small-town businesses and attitude. You won't find chain restaurants here, and you won't find a town trying to cater to corporations or spring breakers or huge events. Flagler Beach does it small, fun and encompasses the town's spirit and makes it a local event.

The Flagler Fiction Series idea became too big for the publisher (I never do anything small), with my vision of 10 short stories set in each unique business, and 2 stories released every Friday and then followed by the complete Print version, and then on to the next place.

I hope the Flagler Beach locals will enjoy seeing some familiar people (they are all fiction, I swear!) and the people who live in other States will find this to be a fun beach read, even if you're staring at cornfields.

As the series progresses and more stories are added, you'll get to follow a few characters through more than one tale, and I hope you find a favorite or three in the myriad characters I've had the privilege of creating... and seeing in my writing travels though Flagler Beach Florida.

Since I began talking to people about doing this contemporary fiction series set in Flagler Beach, so many of them have tossed ideas my way. 'Make sure you add Captain Rob and his golf cart'... 'Make sure the weird guy who walks on the beach late at night gets mentioned'... 'Can you talk about my restaurant or coffee shop or gift shop or...'

But I have enough ideas in my head to fill 100 stories (which is the actual goal once the Flagler Beach Fiction Series is finished), because each and every day I see the many characters who frequent not only Kokomo's Café but the town itself.

You'll find new friends to read about, and might even find a few characters if you are one of my regular readers in the horror and thriller genres.

The story "Girls On The Beach" features Michael Zaun and his friend Larry, who are both from my *Tool Shed* horror novel put out by Angelic Knight Press. Special mention to Stacey Turner for letting me add a sample of the book in the eBook version of the stories, as well.

The couple featured in the story "Maybe I Don't Know?" Real people (to an extent). They sat next to me while I was writing one day, and had pretty much the exact conversation I wrote, but I changed the ending myself and added the plastic cup. In real life, he walked away pissed but relieved she broke up with him and she had a wicked smile on her wrinkled face.

Likewise, "Passing Friend" is based on partial truth. I helped a young girl get away from an abusive boyfriend, and most of the sad facts of it (her name is Ronni) are true. I never had the pleasure of meeting the punk in an alley, although it would have been fun to kick the crap out of him. I let Ike do it for me.

Ike is the creation of local author Tim Baker, a guy I have the pleasure of knowing and hanging out with in and around Flagler Beach. He sets his books (seven and counting) in the area as well, although he writes thrillers. I love his work and love the progression of Ike from a minor character to a huge part of his stories. When I knew I wanted to write the story of Ronni, I knew Ike would be the perfect guy to help her.

I had fun writing the next stories, gotta be honest. First, "It's All About Time" has absolutely nothing to do with real YA ghost author Becky Pourchot. OK, maybe a couple of coincidental things, who can really say? I really liked the character, and beta readers want to see more of her, so expect her to make a cameo or three in future installments. Distracted Reba at J And J Fitness comes to mind.

For those unfamiliar with my horror and zombie work, the Darlene Bobich/John Murphy story "Some Of Your Love"will read like two people happening to meet and the subtle dance they take. What's his real motivation? What's also going through her mind? Will they meet later that night at Golden Lion Café or was it just a purely chance meeting?

If you are a fan of my *Dying Days* zombie series, this was a neat exercise for me to re-imagine the two of them meeting in a non-zombie apocalyptic end of the world scenario. I hope I did both characters justice.

"And Your Dreams Come True" is not based on any real person, although in my mid-20's I did quite a bit of managing bands, and I saw first-hand the craziness of the record industry and the characters who hovered and circled. Danny Street is already turning into an asshole, and he hasn't signed the contract yet.

In "Custom Machine" I took the Black Death MC club from my *Keyport Cthulhu* series and gave them a story, and I love the way Mac spends his time watching them like a hawk.

"Love Is A Woman" was originally conceived weeks ago as an intro to a romantic comedy story from me, something I have never tried. What if two people, from two very different walks of life, coincidentally met? I likened it to a modern day *Grease* but without all the leather jackets and not as much singing. I'm sure Marco and Chelle will be seen again in future Flagler Beach Fiction Series books, and maybe they'll get their own full-length story soon.

The end story, "Here Comes The Night," closes out the day at Kokomo's Café. Wayne Tursha (another character from a previous book I'd written, the thriller *Death Metal*) shows up to sign Danny Street, and you can see where that career is about to head.

I hope you've enjoyed the first peek into the Flagler Beach Fiction Series, and will join me in a few short weeks for part two, *Golden Lion Café*. See you then!

Armand Rosamilia

June 2nd 2013

Armand Rosamilia is a New Jersey boy currently living in sunny Florida, where he spends his hard days soaking up the sun, writing about the people he sees and the monsters in his head, and trying to get writing done when there are so many beautiful distractions in his life...

http://armandrosamilia.com for more information!

TOOL SHED

ARMAND ROSAMILIA